PHOEBE WILL DESTROY YOU

Also by
Blake Nelson

GIRL

BOY

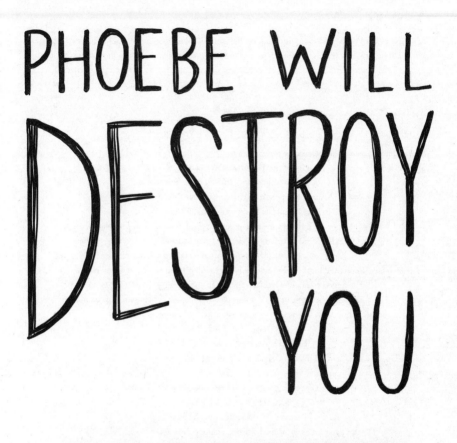

PHOEBE WILL DESTROY YOU

BY BLAKE NELSON

Simon Pulse

New York   London   Toronto   Sydney   New Delhi

SIMON PULSE

An imprint of Simon & Schuster Children's Publishing Division

1230 Avenue of the Americas, New York, New York 10020

First Simon Pulse hardcover edition June 2018

Text copyright © 2018 by Blake Nelson

Jacket photograph of people and beach copyright © 2018 by Anthony Suau

Jacket photograph of sand copyright © 2018 by Thinkstock

For information about special discounts for bulk purchases, please contact Simon & Schuster Special Sales at 1-866-506-1949 or business@simonandschuster.com.

The Simon & Schuster Speakers Bureau can bring authors to your live event. For more information or to book an event, contact the Simon & Schuster Speakers Bureau at 1-866-248-3049 or visit our website at www.simonspeakers.com.

Designed by Sarah Creech

The text of this book was set in Electra LT Std.

Manufactured in the United States of America

2 4 6 8 10 9 7 5 3 1

Library of Congress Cataloging-in-Publication Data

Names: Nelson, Blake, 1960- author.

Title: Phoebe will destroy you / by Blake Nelson.

Description: First Simon Pulse hardcover edition. | New York : Simon Pulse, 2018. | Summary: To avoid his alcoholic mother's problems, Nick, seventeen, stays with his aunt's family near the Oregon coast, where he works at his uncle's car wash and falls into a complicated relationship.

Identifiers: LCCN 2017033159 (print) | LCCN 2017044653 (eBook) | ISBN 9781481488167 (hardcover) | ISBN 9781481488181 (eBook)

Subjects: | CYAC: Dating (Social customs)—Fiction. | Family life—Oregon—Fiction. | Car washes—Fiction. | Alcoholism—Fiction. | Family problems—Fiction. | Oregon—Fiction.

Classification: LCC PZ7.N4328 (eBook) | LCC PZ7.N4328 Pho 2018 (print) | DDC [Fic]—dc23

LC record available at https://lccn.loc.gov/2017033159

For Craig Lesley

"EMPTY MOM"

A car door slammed.

I opened my eyes. I was in the living room, on the couch. I'd fallen asleep.

Mom was home. My mom who'd been in rehab, in California, for three months. My dad had gone to pick her up from the airport, and now they were back. They were in the driveway.

I scrambled to my feet. I shut off the TV. I glanced around at the living room to make sure there weren't any dirty cups or dishes. My dad and I had been cleaning the house all weekend for her homecoming.

I heard voices from outside. I felt that familiar surge of anxiety. *Here comes Mom,* I thought. I stepped over to the hall mirror and checked myself in the reflection. I looked like I always did: longish hair, nervous eyes, seventeen-year-old face.

I had to go greet them. I opened the front door and went outside, into the cold suburban darkness.

My mother didn't look that different. Maybe a little skinnier, a little more gray in her hair. I gave her a quick hug and went around to the trunk and got her suitcase.

I followed the two of them inside. Nobody was talking, I noticed. I carried the suitcase through the living room and into Mom's downstairs office, where she would be sleeping.

Dad went into the kitchen. In a cheerful voice he asked if anyone wanted coffee. I said I'd have some. Mom didn't answer. She stood in the living room looking around at everything. She appeared sort of dazed. She took a seat at the dining room table and checked her phone.

Dad had some pork chops out, to thaw for dinner. He turned on the stove and poured some olive oil in the big skillet. As he did, he told Mom things that had happened while she was gone. The new refrigerator was the main thing. It had a bigger freezer and two doors, which saved electricity. Also, one of our cats, Nipsy, had run away for a week but then come back. Mom didn't really respond to any of this.

Then Allison showed up. She was my mom's best friend. She came in the front door without knocking, and my mom jumped up to greet her. They hugged and gushed, and then Mom grabbed her coat and they went for a walk. That left me and my dad sitting there, with the pork chops cooking.

Mom came back two hours later. She seemed much more emotional now. She gave me a long hug, crying while she held me. But it didn't seem like she was crying for me. It felt more like she was crying for herself, regretting all the ways she had messed up her life and probably thinking about Richard, the guy she was not supposed to see anymore. When she stopped, she cleared away her tears and talked about turning over a new leaf and making a new start, which meant she would be going to AA meetings every night and talking to strange people on the phone. She told us she'd learned certain things about herself, and she was going to be a better wife and mother now.

Dad didn't say anything. He put the pork chops on the table with some green beans and dinner rolls. The pork chops were pretty dried out by now. Mom didn't want hers, so I ate it. She ate some green beans and then made herself some tea. Nobody really talked. Eventually, I said good night and went to my room and fell asleep.

The next day I saw Dr. Snow, my therapist, for a special visit. That was when I said the thing about an "empty mom." It wasn't anything I'd thought about; it just popped out of my mouth. But Dr. Snow kept bringing it up. We talked about it for the next three sessions, what I meant exactly, and what was the *feeling* of "empty mom." But I didn't have an exact feeling about it. I'd just said it. And

I didn't want her to know I'd said it either, because she'd get mad.

So then we tried to live our normal lives, the three of us. Mom would go to work every morning at the university. At night she would go to her AA meetings and then come home and zone out in front of the TV. It was weird having her there. My dad felt it. So did I. I mean, it was better than when she was drinking, and at least we knew where she was. But Mom was bored, you could tell. She wanted to be somewhere else. It made you feel bad, like you weren't good enough and you should be doing something that would make things more interesting for her.

This all happened during the spring of my junior year. I was going to Dr. Snow every Tuesday and Friday, twice the normal sessions. He kept giving me things to do, affirmations to say to myself, breathing exercises to relax. But I was never big on that stuff. Mostly, I stayed after school, playing basketball or working out, avoiding going home.

Eventually, we got to the end of the school year. My friends had various summer activities planned: sports camps, summer jobs, trips to foreign countries. I hadn't made any plans since everything was so focused on my mom. One thing my dad and I agreed on: I needed to get away for the summer. So my dad made some last-minute phone calls. . . .

PART ONE

JUNE

I arrived in Seaside at dusk. The bus let me off on the
side of the highway. There wasn't an official bus stop, just a
bench that said GREYHOUND on it, next to an old gas station that had its windows boarded up and a FOR SALE sign
in the front.

I was supposed to call Aunt Judy when I got there, but
I'd been on the bus for five and a half hours and I didn't feel
like calling right away. It felt good to be outside, in the open
air, in a place that was new and unfamiliar. I walked around
on the crumbly asphalt and stretched my legs. I breathed in
the cool ocean breeze.

There was a store across the two-lane highway called the
Quick-Stop. I waited until the traffic cleared and crossed,
rolling my suitcase behind me. A little bell jingled when I
pushed open the door. The Quick-Stop was a bit run-down:

dirty floors, a sticky soda machine. The beer signs and other advertisements on the walls looked like they'd been there for decades. I walked around, rolling my suitcase up and down the aisles, looking for something to eat. They had some strange stuff in that store: rifles, bear traps, camouflage vests, every kind of knife you could imagine. There was homemade jerky and dried-out corn dogs under a heat lamp. I decided on some Hostess mini donuts and a pint of milk and went to the counter. The creepy lady stared at me while she rang me up. I stared back. She gave me my change, and I rolled my suitcase outside and stood in the parking lot and ate my donuts.

I'd been to Seaside before, visiting the same aunt and uncle, but that was four years ago. My mom didn't like the Reillys, was the reason we hadn't been back for so long.

I didn't remember much about the town. It wasn't very big; I knew that. Across the highway you could see the Coast Range mountains. They'd been clear-cut, and the treeless spots, ragged and bald, looked like a bad buzz job. In the other direction was the Pacific Ocean. You couldn't see it from the Quick-Stop, but you knew it was there. You could smell the salt spray in the air. And the sun had set, so the sky was turning a bright red and pink.

I finished the six donuts. I could have used a couple more, since they were mini donuts and hardly bigger than a bite each. But I didn't buy any more. I drank my milk and watched the cars pulling in and out of the parking lot. I felt good and relaxed for a change, since I was in a new place and I wasn't attached to anybody or anything. Nobody knew me or what my deal was.

I checked my phone. Aunt Judy would be expecting my call. *Just a few more minutes of freedom,* I thought. I watched the Quick-Stop customers. They were mostly local people. Seaside was a pretty rough town, I could see. It wasn't a college town like Eugene, where I lived. None of these people were professors or visiting scholars or college students. But that was okay. Maybe that made it better. Seaside was more rugged; it was a town of loggers and fishermen, more "salt of the earth" types. Maybe I needed some of that in my life.

There were other good things: my aunt and uncle were pretty cool, as far as I could remember. And I'd get to hang out with my cousins, who would be older now. Since I was seventeen, that meant that Kyle was eighteen and Emily was fifteen. Kyle had become a serious baseball player, according to my dad. He'd been given a full scholarship to play for the Oregon State Beavers next year. I didn't know what Emily was into. My main memory of her was she was bossy, and she always had to be the banker when we played Monopoly.

Whatever happened here in Seaside, it would be different. And at least I wasn't home. At least I was far away from whatever trouble might eventually happen with my mom.

I finally called Aunt Judy. Five minutes later a big blue pickup truck pulled into the parking lot of the Quick-Stop. A wide, smiling face appeared in the open window. "Hey, Nick!"

"Hey, Uncle Rob!" I called back. I lifted my rolling suitcase and heaved it into the truck bed. I hurried around to the passenger side. Uncle Rob moved a thermos and some papers off the seat, and I slid into it. I clicked my seat belt on.

He eased the pickup around. "How was the bus ride?"

"It was good," I said, nodding.

Uncle Rob pulled up to the two-lane highway and waited for a break in the traffic. We both watched the passing cars.

"How long did it take?" he asked.

"Five hours," I said. ". . . Five and a half."

When the road cleared, Uncle Rob pushed down on the accelerator. The big truck rumbled onto the highway. It was fun being so high off the ground and looking down on the other cars. I remembered my mom talking about the Reillys, calling them "backwoods" and "rednecks," which was true. But it wasn't necessarily a bad thing, not in my mind.

I snuck a look at Uncle Rob. He looked like a mountain man with his facial scruff and his insulated vest and his oil-stained John Deere cap. The inside of the truck smelled like *men*, like the woods and gasoline and leather boots. It was cool. I liked it.

"And the bus was okay?" he asked.

"Yeah," I said. "It was pretty good. Pretty comfortable seats."

"Which way you go? Up Highway 101?"

"Actually," I said, "we went up the interstate to Portland. And then over."

Uncle Rob nodded.

"That was the boring part," I continued. "Waiting to change buses in Portland. But it was okay. I walked around a little."

Uncle Rob drove. I tried to think of what else I could say about the trip.

"Yeah, this one guy got on in Blanchard," I said. "He didn't smell too good."

Uncle Rob smiled. "That's the Greyhound for you," he said.

"Yeah," I said. I couldn't think of anything else to say.

This was going to be a little weird, I realized. I'd lived my whole life in Eugene, surrounded by the University of Oregon, where my mom was a professor and my dad was a research librarian. We didn't wear John Deere caps or drive pickup trucks in Eugene. We had famous authors over for dinner. The fact that Uncle Rob owned a car wash was another thing my mom made fun of. The Happy Bubble, it was called, which my mom thought was hilarious. She always said that in Oregon, where it rains almost every day, who would go into the car wash business? An idiot, that's who.

We drove along the highway and then turned right, in the direction of the mountains. We wound our way uphill, and then pulled into the gravel driveway of the Reilly residence. I remembered the house from four years ago. It had a sturdy, mountain cabin look to it. A long row of freshly split firewood was stacked along one side.

All the lights were on, I noticed. I hoped the Reillys wouldn't make a big fuss about me coming. My visit had been arranged at the last minute, and I wasn't sure how much they knew about my mom, or how much trouble it would be to have me stay there.

Uncle Rob went in first. I followed behind. We made our way through the living room and into the kitchen. As soon as we entered, Aunt Judy came running over. "Nicholas! Look at you—you're all grown up!" She gave me a big hug and did the looking-me-up-and-down thing. Uncle Rob stood there, grinning. Then this pretty girl got up from the table and came over. I wasn't sure who she was, but I looked closer into her face and realized it was my cousin Emily. "Hi, Nick," she said. She shook my hand and retreated back to her seat.

"Nicholas, you must be starving," said Aunt Judy, drying her hands on a towel. "Did you get a chance to eat anything?"

"Just some mini donuts."

"We'll fix you up," she said, getting some stuff out of the refrigerator. But then she stopped and smiled at me. "It's so nice to see you. We're so glad you're here and that you're staying with us."

"Thanks, Aunt Judy," I said.

Uncle Rob took off his hat and got himself a beer out of the fridge. But then — maybe remembering my mother's problems — he put the beer back and got a Pepsi.

"I'm sorry Kyle isn't here," said Aunt Judy. "He's very excited you'll be here for the summer. You know he's going to Oregon State next year on a baseball scholarship."

"That's what my dad told me," I said.

"You should have been here this spring," said Uncle Rob. "He set the high school strike-out record for the entire Coast League."

I nodded and acted impressed.

Uncle Rob opened his Pepsi and drank some of it. Emily was sitting at the kitchen table looking at her phone.

Aunt Judy offered to make me a sandwich. "What would you like, tuna fish? Or better yet, how about a grilled cheese and some tomato soup? Doesn't that sound good?"

"That sounds great," I said.

"We are so glad to have a little time with our favorite nephew," said Aunt Judy, going back to the refrigerator.

Uncle Rob nodded and smiled and drank more Pepsi.

I stood there awkwardly, nodding along and being properly grateful. I tried to think of what else to say, but I couldn't come up with anything. I looked over at Emily, hoping she could help me out. But she didn't look up from her phone.

The inside of the Reilly house felt like an old ship. The hallways were narrow, and the floorboards were warped and crooked. Maybe because of the sea air? I didn't know.

They didn't have a guest room, so I would be staying in the basement. My aunt and uncle took me down there. Since the house was on a hill, there was a window and a basement door that led outside. Aunt Judy had made the bed up with fresh sheets and blankets. There was a little bookshelf to put stuff in. They had decent Wi-Fi, so that was good. There was a large stand-up freezer on the other side of the room and an exercise bike that looked like it had never been used. The washer and dryer were down there too, which Aunt Judy apologized for. I told her it was okay, I liked falling asleep with a dryer going.

Uncle Rob showed me how the lock on the basement

door worked. The three of us went outside for a minute. Since it was dark now, the stars were out, and the air smelled delicious, like a mixture of the ocean and the forest and burning campfires. It was cold, though. That was something my dad had warned me about. On the coast it stayed cold, even in summer.

Uncle Rob went back upstairs, and Aunt Judy stayed a little longer and helped me put away my clothes. I didn't have much: a pair of Levi's, a couple shirts, a hoodie, a thick wool sweater, and my North Face parka. I had a couple books, including Rilke's *Letters to a Young Poet*, which was my summer reading for AP English. This was supposedly a good book for writers to read, and it was short, so, hopefully, I would get through it by the end of the summer.

After that Aunt Judy went upstairs. So then I was by myself, which was a relief. I continued to settle in. I found an outlet and plugged in my phone. I lay on the bed and looked up at the wood beams and pipes above me. I had a strange feeling then. Like, I knew my aunt and uncle loved me and would be super nice to me, which was great, but really, why was I here? This was a beach town, a tourist town. It kind of didn't make sense. And all the time my dad and I were discussing it, we made it sound like this was what I'd wanted all along. But it wasn't. I came here because of my mom. Because my dad and I were afraid of what might happen, of what she might do. It was like, even when she wasn't doing anything, you had to think about her, you had to account for her. She was always having an effect on you.

I rolled over and tried not to think about it. I was here. I would have to make the best of it. And it was the beach after all. Maybe I could meet some girls. Maybe there would be some fun parties. It was all about your attitude — that's what Dr. Snow always said. It was up to you if you wanted to be happy or not.

3

I saw my cousin Kyle for the first time the next morning. He was eating breakfast at the kitchen table when I emerged from my basement room.

He looked a lot different. He was tall and thick, like a grown man, except that his hair was dyed blond. He looked like what he'd become: a star baseball player with a full scholarship to college. He was still nice, though, and polite. He made room for me at the table and asked me about my school and what sports teams I followed and other things about my life.

Uncle Rob spoke up. "So your dad said you might want to try some shifts at the Happy Bubble this summer?" he said.

I nodded that this was true. "Yeah, if you don't mind."

My dad had recommended this since there wasn't

anything else to do in Seaside. I'd make a little money, and if I didn't work there, I'd just be hanging around the house, and the Reillys would think I was a spoiled rich kid. So we figured I better do it.

So, after breakfast, Kyle, Uncle Rob, and I got in his pickup and drove into town. It was a gray, overcast day, even though it was June. As we drove, I looked out the window at Seaside in the daylight. It wasn't the most beautiful place: a lot of junk in people's yards, and buildings that could use a coat of paint, and car parts and old mattresses stacked up in places. We passed a McDonald's, which, judging by the many cars outside, was the most popular restaurant in town.

The Happy Bubble appeared on the right. It was relatively clean and kept up. The sign had bubbles on it, the largest bubble with a big yellow happy face inside. There were two cars waiting to get washed, one car entering the tunnel and another car behind it. A Happy Bubble employee was spraying the hubcaps and wheels of the waiting car with a hose. It was a white SUV, I noticed, with a family inside and California plates.

"Californians love to wash their cars," Kyle told me.

We pulled into the back parking lot. Kyle already had his gray Happy Bubble shirt on, with a patch that said "Kyle" on it in cursive writing. For pants he had on black Dickies, which the other guys wore also. And black sneakers. So that was the uniform. I would need to get that stuff too.

We parked behind the main building, and I followed Kyle and Uncle Rob into the office. Everything in the place was old: the chairs, the magazines, the notices stuck to the wall behind the counter. It was like the Quick-Stop, worn down but also cozy and familiar in a way. There were donuts in a pink box, and some not very fresh-looking coffee in a coffee maker.

"All right, let's see if we've got a shirt for you," said Uncle Rob, taking me into a storage room. He found a Happy Bubble shirt hanging on a rack. This one said "Chris" on the name patch. He handed it to me; it was a medium and I put it on. It wasn't a perfect fit, but it was close enough. The problem was it was a crappy shirt. 100% polyester. And with threads hanging out on the bottom. It felt scratchy and uncomfortable. But Kyle had the same shirt, and he wasn't complaining. And the guys outside were wearing them. "Yeah," I told Uncle Rob. "That feels about right."

We went back out to the front. There were no more cars, so the sprayer guy, Mike, shut off his hose and took a break. He was older, a grown man, with a mustache and a hardness in his face. He pulled a pack of Marlboros out of his shirt pocket and lit one, holding it clenched in his teeth for a few seconds while he tucked in his shirt.

Kyle showed me how the car wash worked. When a car first pulled up, you sprayed the tires and the hubcaps and along the bottom of the chassis to knock off any mud or dirt. Then, after they paid, you guided them onto a conveyer belt that pulled them through the tunnel. The car needed to be in neutral, and the car windows *had* to be closed. That was the most important thing. Kyle described a couple times when the windows were left open. These were stories that had obviously been told often: a guy getting his sunglasses blasted off by the side sprayer, or the big roller dropping down into a sunroof and yanking off a woman's wig, or a cat jumping out an open window and getting sucked into the vacuum intake (it lived).

Kyle walked me farther into the tunnel and showed me how the machines actually worked. How the big rollers moved against the sides of the car. How the "mitters"—strips of heavy cloth—swept back and forth, cleaning the windshield and the hood. When we got to the other end of the tunnel, I saw that the California SUV was still there. The driver and his family had gone inside, and another Happy Bubble employee, a younger guy, was vacuuming the carpets inside.

"That's Justin," said Kyle. I watched Justin work. It didn't look like fun, getting down on your hands and knees on the wet concrete to vacuum under the seats of somebody's car. No sooner did I think that than Kyle said, "That's probably where my dad will have you start."

4

At twelve thirty Uncle Rob bought everybody lunch from the Freezie Burger down the street. As I sat eating with Kyle, Mike, and Justin, I wondered what my friends at home would think of all this. I wondered what Kate would think.

Kate was my ex-girlfriend. We'd broken up six months before, mostly because things had gotten so intense and we needed a break. That's what we told each other. We'd been together during the worst of my mom stuff and the Richard drama, including the night the cops arrested my dad for punching him in the face in front of our house. I'd slept over at Kate's a couple times when things got too crazy.

Kate probably wouldn't think much of the Happy Bubble scene. She would never say that, of course. She was always supportive. But the idea of me working in a car wash, wearing a crappy uniform shirt, vacuuming old French fries and Cheetos out of people's cars? That wouldn't seem like much of a summer. Especially to her, who would be on Orcas Island with her grandparents, who had a summer house there, and a tennis court and a sailboat.

When I'd finished my cheeseburger, I got out my phone and thought about texting her for some pity points. But I decided not to because that had been part of the problem, too much information on my end, too much burdening her with my family shit. As Dr. Snow said, sometimes people—young people especially—just want to be carefree and not think about other people's problems, not even their boyfriend's. Which I understood.

When my training day was over, instead of riding home with Uncle Rob, I plugged in my headphones and went for a walk into town. Seaside wasn't very big. The busy part was Main Street, which had shops and arcades and bumper cars, and then the Promenade that ran along the beach. The big hotels were closest to the ocean, and behind them were some smaller streets with souvenir stores and restaurants. I found a decent-looking coffee shop a couple blocks inland that was closed. An ice cream shop was open, but it was pretty cold already, so I skipped that. I went ahead to the actual beach.

The beach at Seaside wasn't like what you see on TV. It went for miles and was wide and windy, and the wind gusts blew the sand into your face. I took off my shoes, despite the cold sand, and walked a bit. When I let a wave come up around my feet, it felt like ice water. Still, I kept walking. I went north. It didn't take long until tiny Seaside (population 6,000) disappeared behind me. Then it was just sand and dunes and the mountains to my right, the foaming gray sea to my left. I listened to my music and tried to think what I was going to do here for the entire summer. I had a lot of time to kill.

Eventually, I noticed there were houses above the dunes again, and I could see that I'd come to another town. I checked my phone. *Gearhart*, it said. *Population 1,500.* I saw a trail that led through the dunes. I walked up it and found myself on Gearhart's main road. There were houses, and smaller roads, and a grocery store and a few other shops at the one intersection. Since I was off the beach and sheltered from the wind, it wasn't so cold. It was nice, this little town. The houses were newer and in better shape than in Seaside. The cars were more Volkswagens, Subarus, and BMWs, the kinds of cars you'd see in Eugene.

I went into the store. They had a deli counter with gourmet cheeses and baguettes and Perrier water, the same stuff my mom always made my dad buy. I was hungry, so I ordered a bagel with cream cheese. The woman was very lively, with her lipstick and red apron; she was chatting with the customers about different things. I got my bagel and paid and thanked her.

There was a small park across the street. It was still

light out, so I sat on a bench and ate my bagel. A seagull appeared, and I gave him a tiny bit of it. Then another seagull appeared, and I gave *him* a little bit too. Then about twenty seagulls came crowding around, so I stopped doing that. Instead, I changed benches and watched the people in the park. A well-dressed man was walking his dog. A woman ran by in a jogging outfit. She had sunglasses, spandex pants, something strapped to her bicep. She looked like a Eugene person: blond, slender, and fit.

This was the kind of town Kate's family might stay in. I imagined Kate sitting with me. She would have gotten a salad, something healthy—her mom was big into organic greens. I liked Kate's mother, but we had a difficult history. One of our first encounters was her catching me in their house one night, sleeping in Kate's bed, during one of my mother's drama binges. Kate's mother had freaked out and threatened to call my parents. Kate had to explain to her about my situation at home, and why I was there, and why I couldn't go back to my own house.

Then, a couple weeks later, was the famous night that Richard came to our house looking for my mother and my dad punched him in the face and got taken to jail for assault. After that Kate's mother told me I could stay with them any time I wanted, no questions asked. They even made a little room for me in their basement. At the time I thought how nice of them to help me out. But later, looking back, I could see that was probably the beginning of the end for Kate and me. I mean, Kate's parents didn't want her mixed up in stuff like that. Cop cars and fistfights and the neighbors standing in the street. That was no place for their daughter. Of course they were super nice to me, but it was pretty clear the message Kate was getting: *Is this the kind of family you want to be part of?*

5

I bought my black Dickies pants the next day, before my first official shift at the Happy Bubble. I got them at Bill's Army-Navy shop, which was hidden behind one of the souvenir stores off Main Street. I also found some cheap ($9.99) black sneakers, since that's what the other guys wore. The shoes didn't even have a brand; they just said "Made in China" on the insole.

Then I stopped by the coffee shop down the street and got a caffe latte with almond milk. The coffee at the Happy Bubble hadn't looked so great. Also, I liked being in a real coffee shop, with real espresso smells like the cafés in Eugene. But when I got to the Happy Bubble, Mike, the older guy, looked at my coffee-to-go cup and frowned. Like, who was I that I couldn't drink the regular coffee? He and Justin were eating glazed donuts, so I ate one too, to show I wasn't a total snob. Then we all sat around and waited for customers. It was cold and wet outside; a mist was coming in off the ocean, so nobody was going to get their car washed probably. I said that to Mike, but he shrugged and said that people still got their cars washed. He didn't know why, maybe because they were on vacation and didn't know what else to do with themselves.

Mike went outside for a smoke. Justin scrolled up and down on his cracked phone screen. Uncle Rob eventually called and told us to clean in the tunnel, which was what you did during times with no customers. I mostly stuck with Justin during this. He seemed nicer than Mike, who never stopped smoking. Even when he was doing complicated things with his hands, Mike would still be clenching a cigarette between his teeth and squinting as the smoke went in his eyes.

I tried to talk to Justin while we wiped the gunk out of the machines. I thought he'd said he went to Seaside High School with Kyle, but now his story was slightly different; he was a year older than Kyle and perhaps hadn't actually graduated. He didn't seem eager to clarify, so I didn't bother him about it.

I also asked Justin about his left hand, which was missing two fingers. The pinky was totally gone, and the ring finger was about an inch-long stub. He didn't want to talk about that, either. "Hunting accident," he finally said. It freaked me out a little, watching him hold things. Sometimes when he gripped the vacuum hose, his left hand looked like a claw. At one point he disappeared for a few minutes, and when he came back, he smelled like weed. This didn't surprise me.

In the afternoon, the sun came out and we got a few customers. Kyle was in charge, and he told me to work with Justin, vacuuming and cleaning people's windows. So I did that. It cost extra to get your car vacuumed so not everyone did it. But most people did.

The good part of vacuum duty was how powerful the vacuum was. It would suck up everything in the car if you weren't careful. "Ya gotta get used to it," said Justin, yelling over the sound of it. I was struggling to vacuum a minivan. The hose kept getting stuck to the floor. You'd pull really hard to get it off, and it would get stuck to the seat. Then it would get stuck to you, sucking up your arm hairs or half your shirt. It was also extremely loud, so I couldn't hear what Justin was telling me as it swallowed three quarters and a small *Star Wars* figure out of somebody's cup holder.

"What do we do about spare change?" I yelled to Justin from under the dashboard.

"Suck it up," he yelled back. "We'll dig it out later. We'll split it."

"Do the customers care?"

He shrugged. "Not that I ever noticed."

I saw another cluster of dimes and pennies, and reluctantly sucked them up.

"If they really wanted it, they'd pick it up, right?" reasoned Justin.

"I guess so," I said.

I pulled back the floor pad and uncovered two more quarters and a nickel and a dime. I looked over at Justin. He pointed to suck them up. So I did.

I got off at five that day and walked into town again. It was still sunny out; the streets were full of tourists. I stopped by the coffee shop and got a piece of crumb cake. I was wondering if anyone my age ever hung out at the coffee shop, but it didn't seem like it. It was mostly old people or clueless tourists standing around, blocking the line and not knowing what a macchiato was.

After that I walked the 2.4 miles back to the Reillys' and took a shower. I was pretty dirty from crawling around on the wet cement with my vacuum hose. I'd got some machine grease on my arm somehow and had to scrub it super hard to get it off.

But overall it felt good to put in a full day's work and be pleasantly tired afterward. It made me feel like a real adult. Also, the vibe of the Happy Bubble, it wasn't like folding sweaters at the Gap. It was a working-man's job. Heavy machinery was involved. And hard physical labor. Which made it more satisfying in a way.

When I was all clean, I went down to my basement room and texted Kate. I told her about my first days in Seaside, making fun of it a little, which she usually appreciated. That was one thing she liked about me, I could always make her laugh.

Later, I went upstairs for dinner, which was mac and cheese and Aunt Judy's special meat loaf, which was delicious. Then I watched the Mariners baseball game with Kyle and Uncle Rob. This wasn't the most exciting thing, but I liked hearing Uncle Rob and Kyle talk about baseball strategy. They knew a lot about it.

The first social thing I did in Seaside was with Emily.
That was on Saturday night. Kyle was at Oregon State for
the weekend; he was already working out with his college
baseball team, even though he'd just graduated from high
school three weeks before. So Emily got stuck with me. She
was going with some friends to a movie, and her mother
suggested they take me along.

I thought Emily had been avoiding me a little. Not that I
blamed her. She was fifteen, and it was probably awkward to
have her boy cousin suddenly show up and be living in her
house and taking showers in her shower.

Since her mother told her to invite me, I made an excuse
to let Emily off the hook. But Aunt Judy heard me and yelled
from the kitchen that she needed me to go, because I could
drive. So then I had to.

I drove Emily in Aunt Judy's Toyota. We stopped at another house to pick up her three friends: Jace, Kelsey, and Lauren. They came running out of the house and jumped into the back seat.

"Jace!" said Kelsey, as they squeezed in. "Are you going to text Zach or not!?"

"I told you, I'm not!" said Jace, who was the tallest of the three.

"But you have to!" insisted Lauren. "He talked to you at the party. This is your chance!"

"You guys have to put your seat belts on," I said from the driver's seat.

The three girls dug around for their seat belts.

"But I don't know what to say!" said Jace.

"Say anything," said Lauren. "Ask him what he's doing tonight."

"But he'll think I like him!" said Jace.

"But you *do* like him!"

"You have to do something," said Kelsey. "Or nothing will ever happen."

"Willa Flores isn't afraid to text boys," said Lauren. "And now she's with Luke."

Everyone agreed that Willa Flores had the right approach. From the silence, I assumed Jace was typing something.

"What did you write?" asked Kelsey.

"I wrote, *what's up.* But then I deleted it."

"Jace, you have to do this!"

"But I can't!"

"Give me your phone!"

"NO! GIVE IT BACK! Jeez, you guys!"

"He might like you. What if he likes you, and you don't do anything? You'll regret it for the rest of your life!"

"If he liked me, then he would text *me*, not the other way around!" said Jace.

"You have to *make* boys like you," said Lauren.

I pulled into the Cineplex parking lot. We were early, so I took my time looking for a parking spot.

"So what do I say?"

"Say: *Hey, Zach. What's up? We're going to the movies.*"

"Just that?"

"Yes, just that."

"But it doesn't ask him anything," said Jace. "It's not a real question."

"It doesn't have to be a real question. You're just starting a conversation."

"You guys sound like fifth graders," said Emily. She was in the front seat beside me and hadn't spoken through any of this. "Just write the stupid text and shut up about it!"

There was a brief silence as Jace typed into her phone.

"Okay . . . ," said Kelsey. "Now press send."

"I can't," said Jace.

"Just do it."

"Okay, I will," said Jace. "Don't touch me!"

"Send! Hit send!"

"Okay, okay. Gawd. I did it, it's done!"

There was a great sigh of relief from the three girls.

"Can we please go see the movie now?" said Emily.

We went inside, bought our tickets, and made our way into the theater. But once inside, I realized nobody cared at all about the movie. As soon as the previews started, Kelsey and Lauren jumped up and ran back to the lobby.

"Where are they going?" I whispered to Emily.

"They saw some people they know," she said.

Ten minutes later they came back. But then after some texting, some whispering, and some arguing, they jumped back up and went to the lobby again.

Jace, meanwhile, was checking her phone for a response from Zach. Emily was also on her phone and then got up and went to the lobby as well, missing the first fifteen minutes of the movie.

Everyone kept coming and going. At one point I was the only one in my seat. I tried to be cool and not worry about it. Eventually Emily and Jace came back, but when the movie finally ended, Kelsey and Lauren were still gone.

"Uh, where did your friends go?" I asked Emily. She didn't answer, and now Jace was freaking out because it had been two hours and Zach had not texted her back. She looked like she might cry.

I was more worried about Kelsey and Lauren. I didn't know what went on in Seaside. Was it normal for two fifteen-year-old girls to vanish from a movie theater on a Saturday night?

When we got outside, I made Emily and Jace walk around the parking lot afterward, looking for her missing friends. Sure enough, we found them sitting in the back seat of a beat-up Camaro with two very sketchy dudes who looked like they were several years out of high school. These guys wore flat-brimmed hats and basketball jerseys and had wispy beards and mustaches. The car was full of cigarette smoke, with the clear smell of weed mixed in. I was still trying to act casual, but inside I was like, *What if something happens to them? I brought them here!*

Nobody else seemed concerned. Emily started talking to the guys like they were old friends, which it turned out they were. She introduced them to me.

"Nick, this is Wyatt and Carson," she said.

I bent down to look inside the car. The two guys were so stoned their eyes barely opened. "Nice to meet you," I said.

"'Sup," said the nearest one.

Emily wanted to leave. She started walking back to our car; reluctantly I followed.

"So we're leaving Kelsey and Lauren?" I asked.

"Yes," said Emily.

"And they can get home? Those guys are okay . . . ?"

"They're fine," said Emily, giving me a look.

So that's what we did. We left Kelsey and Lauren with the two thugs in the Camaro.

Jace, Emily, and I started to drive back to Jace's house, but then the two girls decided they wanted to go to the

Sandpiper instead. I followed their directions, and we pulled into a restaurant that was basically a Denny's with a beach theme.

We sat at a table, and Jace immediately checked again for a text back from Zach, which had not come. She shook her head. "Oh my God, now he'll tell people how I text him and bother him and stalk him!"

"No he won't," said Emily. "And what do you care about Zach? Do you even like him, or did Lauren talk you into it?"

Jace put down her phone. "I don't know," she said. "Maybe I don't like him."

The waitress came and wiped down our table with a dirty rag, which made it greasier than it already was. Then she brought waters, and we drank them and talked about the movie that nobody saw. I asked about the two guys in the car, Wyatt and Carson. Jace said they were from Astoria and that the boys up there sometimes came down to Seaside to party and hang out.

"They didn't seem a little sketchy to you?" I asked.

"They're fine," said Jace. "They just get bored. Astoria is pretty small."

"We do the same thing," said Emily. "We go up there."

"What about Gearhart," I said, remembering the little town I had stumbled on.

Both girls looked at me, then at each other. "What do you know about Gearhart?" asked Jace.

"Nothing," I said. "I just walked up the beach and ended up there."

"That's a long walk," said Emily.

"It wasn't that long," I said.

"That's where the rich people live," said Jace. "And the old people."

I nodded. "Yeah, that's what it looked like."

"I like going up there," said Jace. "I'm not afraid of rich people."

Emily wasn't saying anything, I noticed. She was reading her menu.

"What's Eugene like?" Jace asked me.

I thought of how to answer. I realized I'd been in Seaside for almost a week, and nobody had said a word to me about Eugene, or even asked me where I was from.

"It's a college town," I said.

"What does that mean?"

"There's college kids everywhere, for most of the year. And lots of stuff for students. Coffee shops, organic restaurants, bookstores . . ."

"I would love to go to University of Oregon," said Jace.

"Yeah, it's pretty cool," I said. "My mom teaches there, so I get in free to the pool or the library or whatever."

"I hate Seaside," said Jace.

"Don't say that," said Emily.

"Why not?" said Jace. "It's true. Seaside is such a hick town. We don't even know what hicks we are."

"I'm not a hick," said Emily.

"Yes you are," said Jace. "You just don't know it."

"I've been to Portland a million times," said Emily.

"*Portland*," scoffed Jace. "That's just a bigger hick town. I want to go to New York."

"I like Seaside," I said. "I like how earthy it is."

"You're just saying that," said Jace. "I'm getting out of here the minute I graduate. And I'm never coming back."

"What happened to Zach?" said Emily.

Jace got out her phone and checked again. "Still nothing. Oh my God, I can't believe I let those guys talk me into that. He's totally ignoring me!"

"It doesn't matter," said Emily. "It was just a friendly text."

"Of course it matters. He knows why I texted him."

"Don't be so sure. Zach's pretty dumb."

Jace frowned. "He *is* kinda dumb, isn't he?" she said. At that moment a huge plate of half French fries, half onion rings arrived.

"Sounds like it's for the best," I said, reaching for the ketchup.

Later, after we dropped off Jace, it was just Emily and me in the car. "So those are my friends," said Emily.

"They seem nice," I said.

"I don't like it when Jace says things against Seaside," said Emily. "I mean, everyone's entitled to their opinion. I just don't think you should say stuff about where you live."

"She wants to see the world, I guess."

Emily said nothing. She stared out the window for a while. Then she got out some gum and gave me a piece, and we chewed gum the rest of the way home.

7

The next day it was sunny again, and things got busy at the Happy Bubble. At noon I was sent to Freezie Burger to get everyone lunch. Freezie Burger was an old-school fast food place with chrome counters and big windows and red plastic picnic tables outside. The girls who worked there probably all went to Seaside High. They wore little white aprons and hats and wrote your order on a pad like the old days.

My order was pretty simple: four Cheeseburger Deluxes, two with fries, two with onion rings. I could see the girls noticing my Happy Bubble shirt. You could tell they were curious who I was. A new boy in town! But they didn't say anything. They just smiled a certain way. And made sure to pack my order carefully and with lots of extra napkins.

* * *

When I returned to the Happy Bubble, there was a guy in a van waiting to go into the tunnel. Another car was behind him. No one was helping them. I hurried into the office and put the lunch bags down. Nobody was in there, either. Then I heard laughing from the back parking lot. I opened the back door and saw Kyle, Justin, and Mike all standing around an open-top Jeep with two girls inside. The driver was blond and was grinning and laughing at something Kyle was saying. She said something back, and everyone cracked up.

I wondered if I should interrupt or just go help the customers myself. But that wasn't my job—I was on vacuum duty—and I didn't know how to take people's credit cards.

So I walked out toward the Jeep. Everyone was focused on the blond girl in the driver's seat. She was wearing fluorescent pink short-shorts and a white hoodie. The guys were joking with her. Justin grabbed the roll bar with his three-fingered hand and climbed up into the back seat, like he was going to drive off with them. But they shooed him away and he jumped out.

"All right, we gotta go," said the blonde. She started to pull forward, but the Jeep had a stick shift and it jerked once and died. "I still don't know how to drive this stupid thing!" she said. Kyle reached over her bare legs, grabbed the stick shift, and jammed it forward. "Now you're in first."

"Oh my Gawd . . . ," said the girl. "Do that again!"

Everyone laughed.

She let out the clutch and the car lurched forward,

stopped again and then bounced out of the parking lot and into the street.

As the Jeep sped away, the guys turned back toward the office, laughing and grinning to themselves. Then they saw me gesturing that there were customers waiting. Mike and Kyle quickly ran around to the front, where they apologized and called everyone "sir" and "ma'am" the way Uncle Rob likes us to.

Justin and I went into the office. We still had a couple minutes before anyone would need a vacuum. Justin pulled his cheeseburger out of the bag and unwrapped it.

"Who were those girls in the Jeep?" I asked.

"That was Nicole," said Justin, without looking up. "Nicole and Phoebe."

"They looked like fun."

"Ha-ha," he said, taking a big bite of his Freezie Burger. "They *are* fun," he said with his mouth full. "They're *lots* of fun."

We were busy all afternoon. At one point there were five cars waiting in line. Justin and I vacuumed nonstop. Sometimes we'd work on the same car together. I'd crawl in from the passenger side and grab any loose garbage: empty water bottles, Big Mac containers, crumpled potato chip bags. Then Justin would come in with the vacuum and suck up whatever was left. He found a five-dollar bill under the seat of one car. He showed it to me and then slipped it into his pocket. As he promised, at the end of our shift we went through the vacuum dust bag and dug out all the change. On that day it added up to $12.20, which we split.

"Beer money," said Justin.

After work Justin and I ended up walking together to the Promenade. He stopped at a little market off Main Street and came out with a brown paper bag. He held the bag open so I could look in. There was a six-pack of cold sixteen-ounce Budweisers inside and a pint bottle of Jim Beam whiskey. He was clearly not old enough to buy liquor. "Wow," I said. "How'd you manage that?"

"I got ways," he said.

We walked to the circular viewing area at the center of the Promenade, and then down the stairs to the actual sand. I followed Justin as he circled around under the stairs and plopped himself in the shade. I wasn't sure what his plan was, but I sat beside him. We were out of sight of the Promenade, but the people on the beach could still see us clearly, sitting there under the stairs. He reached into the bag and handed me one of the beers.

I took the beer and wasn't sure what to do with it. Open it? Here? Where everyone on the beach could see us? There were little kids kicking a ball right in front of us.

"Don't worry, we're safe," said Justin. "The cops can't see us."

He cracked his beer open and took a drink. Then he opened the whiskey.

I opened my beer too and took a couple sips. This was

weird, though. We were like a couple of bums, hiding out beneath the stairs, drinking whiskey in broad daylight.

Justin didn't seem to have any problem with it. I watched his three-fingered hand while he took a deep chug of the whiskey. Then he offered me some. I still had to go home and eat dinner with the Reillys. I couldn't show up drunk. So I waved the whiskey away and took another small sip of my beer.

"So Nicole, the girl in the Jeep . . . ," I asked Justin. "What's her deal?"

"She's in love with Kyle."

"She and everyone else," I said.

"'Cept she used to have him."

"She did? Like how?"

"Like they were together," said Justin. "A couple years back. They were a big thing."

"But not now?"

"He moved on," he said.

"And she didn't?"

Justin shrugged. "You saw it."

"Yeah, I guess I did."

I took another small sip of my beer. The little kids kicked their ball in my direction. I reached over and grabbed it and threw it back to them. They stared at us for a second. We still had our Happy Bubble shirts on, which didn't seem like the best advertisement for the car wash, two teenaged employees, hiding out under the stairs, drinking Jim Beam like a couple of alcoholics. But it appeared that Justin did this all the time. And I didn't want to insult him. So I drank a little more of my beer and sat for a few more minutes. Then I said I had to get going. I was about to throw the rest of my beer in the trash can, but Justin saw that it was still mostly full. "Hey, don't toss that," he said. "It's a sin to waste good beer."

I nodded that it was and handed over my Budweiser can. Then I got the hell out of there.

By now I'd been in Seaside for two weeks, but I still hadn't had a real conversation with Kyle. I felt bad about that. We'd been close as little kids. And since I was an only child, he'd been the closest I'd ever had to a brother.

I assumed he knew—and Emily, too—that the reason I was there was because of my mom. They never said anything, though. This made things awkward between the three of us. Like, were we really going to pretend I was in Seaside for some other reason? Because I loved the beach so much? Or was eager to pursue my car-vacuuming career?

But really, Kyle was just too busy to think about his long-lost cousin. He was driving back and forth to Oregon State for his baseball workouts, and at the end of the summer he'd be moving there to start school. He supposedly had a new girlfriend, Britney, who I hadn't seen. This was according to Justin, who told me Britney would get dumped when Kyle left for Oregon State, and that everyone knew it and felt sorry for her. She was hanging on to her last precious months with Kyle, which I guess any Seaside girl would do, if she were in her place.

It was weird, that part of it, how insanely popular Kyle was. The best looking, the best athlete, every girl in love with him. And the locals so proud of him, people coming into the car wash, wanting to shake his hand or stare at him or tell him how great he is. And meanwhile, he's still wearing his crappy Happy Bubble shirt and hosing the mud off their hubcaps. Even Aunt Judy was in awe of him, and Uncle Rob definitely was, though he tried to cover it up with his "bro vibe," like he and Kyle were more best friends than father and son.

Kyle handled it well, I thought. I didn't know if I could deal with people gawking at me like that. It just sucked that I couldn't spend time with him in any normal way. But I guess that's what happens when you become a big star. Everyone wants your attention, your time, your acknowledgment. And all the while, you're trying to keep your head clear and stay focused on whatever your great talent is— throwing a baseball really hard, in Kyle's case.

Since I hardly saw Kyle, I talked to Emily instead, or I tried to. It got a little easier after we went to the movie that night. At least she knew I wasn't going to embarrass her around her friends. We watched TV together when there wasn't a baseball game. She had her shows she liked, *The Bachelor* and some others. I would sit on the couch, across from her, and look at stuff on my phone or try to read *Letters to a Young Poet*.

We were sitting together one night, when I asked what happened with Jace and Zach.

"He never texted her back," said Emily.

"That's too bad," I said.

"Zach is in demand," said Emily, not looking away from the TV. "He has a lot of options."

"He can have any girl he wants?"

"Not *any* girl . . . ," said Emily.

"Who will he choose?" I asked.

"Probably Taylor Kittman. She's supposedly the prettiest girl in our class."

"So that's the main thing? He wants the prettiest girl?"

"Yeah. I mean, she's nice, too. She's nice to boys at least."

"Sounds like my school."

"Jace is too tall for him, I think," said Emily.

"She is kinda tall," I said, remembering Jace. She was good-looking, in her way. But she wasn't the type a truly popular guy would go for. Not at my school, and probably not at Seaside.

"Do you like tall girls?" asked Emily. She didn't look at me when she said it.

"Me?" I said. "No. I mean, I don't *not* like them."

Emily remained focused on the TV. *The Bachelor*

wasn't on that night, so we were watching *MasterChef*.
"Do you have a girlfriend?" she asked.

"No."

"Did you ever?"

"Yeah. This girl, Kate."

This seemed to interest Emily. She tried not to show it,
though. "How long did you go out for?"

"Ten months, three weeks, four days."

"Wow. You really keep track."

"At my school making it to a year is a huge thing. We
came pretty close. But you know. Once it's over, it's over."

"Did she break up with you, or did you break up
with her?"

"It was pretty mutual."

"People say that," said Emily. "But it's never mutual."

"She broke up with me," I said. "She was sick of my
family stuff."

Emily didn't respond. This was the first mention of my
family between us. I wanted to say something else, to show
her it was no big deal, that I didn't mind talking about it.
But I couldn't think of what.

Aunt Judy was the easiest of the Reilly family to talk to.
Sometimes I'd hang out with her in the kitchen. She'd
chatter away about whatever: local gossip; town politics;
the old widow who owned the flower store. Or tourist
stuff she thought I might be interested in: surfing lessons,

or horseback riding on the beach, or a zip line someone was building in the mountains.

At one point I got a fairly long e-mail from my dad, telling me the news from home. So then I relayed this information to Aunt Judy while we were cleaning up after dinner: how mom was still sober, and going to her Alcoholics Anonymous meetings, and getting her classes ready for the fall semester.

"She still has her job?" said Aunt Judy with amazement. "After all that?"

I nodded. This was one of my mother's many talents. She somehow never got fired, no matter what crazy things she did.

I asked Aunt Judy what my dad was like when he was a teenager. She told me how he threw this giant senior party the last month of high school, with ten kegs and a live band; it was this legendary thing. Their parents weren't home of course, and it got out of hand, and then the police came and everyone got busted. Still, it was considered the best party of the year, my dad was considered a hero. The yearbook even devoted a whole spread of pictures to it.

My aunt Judy was loading the dishwasher as she told me this. She said, "Your dad always had a lot of friends in high school. And also in college. He was very popular in those days, and very happy. . . . People loved him—they looked up to him." A serious look came over her face. "He seems very different now. He isn't really himself."

I nodded. She was obviously talking about being with my mom.

"But that happens to everyone," she said, quickly changing her tone. She stood up straight and dried her hands with a towel. "You change when you get married. And when you have children. You become more serious. You have to. It's perfectly normal."

Justin and I continued to bond as the vacuum crew. We worked well together. A car came out of the tunnel, and, depending on what kind of car it was and how dirty, we divided our labors and went to work: cleaning the windows, vacuuming the carpets, wiping out the cup holders and other dashboard nooks—in most cases finishing an entire car in under two minutes. I always liked being good at a job, even a crappy job. Justin seemed to be that way too. And so the two of us quietly killed it, car after car, day after day.

Then one afternoon Nicole and Phoebe showed up again in the Jeep. Everyone snuck out to the back parking lot to bask in the glow of Nicole's sexy smile. This time I watched the other girl, Phoebe, as well. She was quieter and definitely more "the friend," but she was also cute in her own way, and had a more alternative style.

Nicole had come to tell Kyle some urgent piece of news, which turned out to be nothing. While that was going on, Phoebe climbed out of the Jeep and came toward the office to use our restroom. I was hanging back, standing by the back door in case any customers came. I watched Phoebe approach. She had a pretty face, despite her dyed black hair and overly pale complexion. She didn't look at me. She wasn't paying attention to anything, really. She looked bored, or oblivious, I guess.

When she got to the door, I moved out of her way. Normally I wouldn't talk to a girl like that, but for some reason I felt like I could. "Hey," I said.

She glanced once at my face.

"I'm Nick," I said.

"Hi, Nick," she said, going past me. I started to direct her to the bathroom, but she already knew the way.

When she came back out a few minutes later, she walked past me again. I politely moved aside and watched her walk back to the Jeep. She had an interesting walk. She was interesting in general. There was definitely something about her.

Later, as we cleaned the windows of a large RV, Justin told me that Phoebe and Nicole had graduated from high school that spring, with Kyle. So they were a grade older than me. I was relieved to hear that. It made it okay for me to have crushes on them. I didn't have to worry they would like me back. Since I was just a kid to them.

*　*　*

Besides coworkers, Justin and I were starting to become friends. I had to be careful, though; I didn't want to become *too* good of friends with someone who got drunk under the Promenade stairs in plain sight of everyone. It was a difficult situation. He started asking me to come hang out with him and his friends after work. Usually I'd make up some excuse. But he kept asking, and, finally one Friday, I said okay.

We drove up to Tillicum, which was another small town up the coast. We stopped off to get beer and then continued in Justin's crappy Ford Focus. (He couldn't even put it through the car wash because the passenger window wouldn't stay up.)

In Tillicum, we followed the one paved road to a dirt road, and followed that to a small, falling-down house deep in the woods. We got out, and I swear, it was like the Garden of Eden in there, quiet and peaceful, the late afternoon sun shining down through the gaps in the trees. You could even hear a babbling brook somewhere. That was the thing about the Oregon coast. So much natural beauty, and then in the middle of it there'd be an old rusted washing machine lying on its side with its tubes and wires hanging out.

That's kind of what the house was like—the window frames coming apart, moss on the roof, junk around the outside. We went to the front door and Justin knocked. When nobody answered, he pushed the door open with his shoulder.

It was a mess inside as well: computer crap, gamer stuff, cords, wires, screens everywhere. Justin called out, and this huge guy appeared. He must have weighed three hundred pounds. He was in shorts and a dirty T-shirt and flip-flops. His name was Calhoun. We gave him a beer, and the three of us sat in his trashed living room. Justin told him I was Kyle Reilly's cousin and I was working at the Happy Bubble this summer. Calhoun seemed impressed. So we talked about that for a while: the car wash and how you could meet girls there, and the different kinds of girls you might meet. Calhoun had a lot to say about girls, so we kept on with that: what California girls were like versus Oregon girls, how Seaside girls compared to Portland girls, which girls were snobs and which might want to fool around, and how you could tell, and what the signs were, and what was the best thing to say to a girl, depending on what your intentions were, et cetera, et cetera.

Calhoun was doing all the talking, and eventually I stopped listening and found myself thinking about Phoebe and the moment she walked by me at the Happy Bubble. *Hi, Nick,* she had said. It was very cool, her tone of voice, but not entirely unfriendly, either. Would I talk to her again if I saw her? Maybe. Though I couldn't imagine a girl like Phoebe being interested in me. I would be too boring for her. She and Nicole, they were party girls, wild girls; they drove around in an open Jeep, flirting with guys like Kyle. On the other hand, this was Seaside. It was a small town; maybe things were different here. Maybe the normal rules didn't apply.

*   *   *

I was halfway through my first beer when Calhoun reached behind his recliner chair and pulled out the biggest bong I had ever seen. It was four feet tall. It was so big, it seemed impossible a human could actually smoke out of it.

But they did. Calhoun fired it up, and he and Justin started taking gigantic bong hits. I sat watching. That bong looked lethal. I started telling them I didn't want any, I was good, I had small lungs, but Calhoun looked deeply hurt and offended. So then I thought I could probably survive a very small hit. So I tried that, sucking up what I thought was the tiniest possible amount of smoke. But even that burned into my chest like a hot iron. I immediately started coughing and choking and pounding on my sternum. Calhoun and Justin thought this was hilarious. Then they took more gigantic hits themselves. I couldn't believe they could smoke more.

After that we drank more beer. I needed the cold liquid to soothe my scalded throat. So now, not only was I totally high, I was pretty drunk, too. Then I realized it was almost eight, and Aunt Judy would wonder where I was. I dug out my phone and texted her that I was going to eat with Justin and hang out with him that night. She texted back right away saying that was fine, they wouldn't wait for me.

So that was easy. And now I was free to do whatever. I opened another beer.

After the bong hits, the conversation was mostly laughing and saying random things. Justin talked about how trees communicate with each other through energy fields. Calhoun had read something about how long a human would remain conscious in outer space without a space suit. Three seconds, he claimed. Which would give you time to really experience the vastness of the universe. Unfortunately, your brain would then be freeze-dried by the cold. Or would explode, depending on the exact conditions. Still, reasoned Calhoun, that wouldn't be a bad way to "go out."

Driving back to Seaside, I was so drunk and stoned I literally couldn't see straight. When we waited at an intersection, I tried to focus on the traffic light, but found it kept veering off to the right.

There was no way I could go back to the Reillys' like that, so I told Justin to let me off at the Promenade. When he pulled over, I couldn't figure out how to get my door open. When I did get out, I didn't know where I was. I was *lost* in downtown Seaside, which had, like, two main streets. I stumbled around and managed to find the Beach Mart, where I bought a two-liter bottle of water. Somehow I made it back to the Promenade, where I flopped on a bench. I stayed there, paralyzed basically, drinking water and waiting for the worst of my drunkenness to pass.

A couple hours later I began the 2.4-mile walk home. It was very late when I found myself in front of my basement door. I was still drunk and tried desperately to be quiet, which was hard in the dark, with the key and the creaky old door. When I finally got in, I quickly took off my clothes and crawled into bed before anyone could come down and ask me any questions.

Sure enough, the minute I pulled the covers over my head, the upstairs door opened. Someone came partway down the steps.

"Nick?" said a soft voice. It was Emily. Thank God.

I lifted my head out of the covers. "Oh. Hi," I said.

"Are you okay?"

"Yeah, I think so."

"It's two-thirty a.m."

"I know. Did I wake everyone up?"

"No. I was already awake."

I looked up at her. "I am so drunk right now," I said.

"Where did you go?"

"I was hanging out with Justin."

"Well that explains it," she said. She was sitting on the steps with her elbows on her knees. "Are you okay?"

"I don't know. The bed is starting to spin."

"If you have to puke, you can go in that basin by the washing machine."

"Okay. Thanks."

"How did you get home?"

"Walked."

She remained sitting on the stairs for another few moments.

Then she stood up. "Okay well, good night," she said, heading back up the stairs.

"Good night."

The next morning, Uncle Rob called down to my base-
ment room that Kyle was going to be working out at the high
school, before the car wash opened, if I wanted to come
watch him pitch.

After everything I'd heard, of course I did, despite probably the worst hangover I'd ever had in my life. I stumbled
out of bed and put on my pants and climbed up the stairs.
The first floor was bustling with activity. Aunt Judy was
cooking, Kyle was eating, Uncle Rob was calling people
on his phone. There was an open cooler by the door with
bags of ice and some Gatorade in it. There were two large
buckets spilling over with baseballs and a plastic tub filled
with other assorted gear, as well as a gym bag, a duffel bag,
and some electronic stuff. Kyle, I noticed, was wearing
brand-new orange-and-brown Nike sweats with the little

beaver head that was the mascot of Oregon State.

Kyle working out was a big deal, apparently.

After breakfast, the three of us loaded up the truck. We drove to the highway and then north to Seaside High School. We pulled around to the baseball field. It wasn't much to look at. Brown grass. Rickety bleachers. There were already several cars in the parking lot, and some guys standing by the backstop. These people turned out to be Kyle's teammates from his high school team the year before. They were happy to show up, if Kyle needed a workout. They all came right over to say hi to Uncle Rob. There was a lot of back-slapping and teasing Kyle about his fancy sweat pants and Nike gear.

Kyle and his teammates spread out across the grass to stretch. This went on for about ten minutes. Then everyone partnered up and played catch. I threw the ball back and forth with Uncle Rob. The fuzziness in my brain was beginning to clear.

Eventually, Kyle made his way to the pitcher's mound and began throwing practice pitches to a guy in a catcher's outfit. He did this for another five minutes, stopping occasionally to chat with people or fiddle with his glove or adjust his hat.

One of the guys put on a batting helmet and batting gloves and began taking practice swings. Kyle was pitching a little faster now, and with a little more force. Uncle Rob pulled out an expensive-looking radar gun and started checking his speed. He yelled out to Kyle: "Seventy-one!" "Sixty-eight!" "Seventy-five!" I was standing behind the backstop, watching all this through the fence. Kyle's warm-up pitches cut through the air with a pleasing sizzle sound. And they came fast. *SLAP!* went the catcher's glove, a little cloud of dust coming off it with the impact. And Kyle wasn't even throwing at full speed yet.

So then everyone paused for a minute while the first batter strode to the plate. He was nervous, you could see, but also trying very hard to appear confident. He tapped the tip of the bat against home plate a couple times and then backed away, taking a deep breath and crossing himself.

Some of the other guys had run out into the field with their baseball mitts, to field any balls that got hit. A couple more guys began swinging bats and getting ready to take their turn against Kyle. Meanwhile, about a dozen younger kids had shown up on bikes and gathered beside me behind the backstop. They were chattering excitedly among themselves. "That's Kyle Reilly!" I heard one say.

I had noticed a steady stream of cars pulling into the parking lot since we arrived. Now, when I looked behind me, I saw an actual crowd had gathered. People were sitting in the bleachers. Nobody wanted to miss this. People were texting their friends.

The guy with the batting helmet stepped back to the plate. A tingle of excitement passed through the crowd. People started to yell stuff. The catcher got down in his stance and everyone became very serious. Kyle stared at the batter. Then he wound up in a slow deliberate motion, turned away from us for a moment, then uncoiled himself in a fast, fluid flow. The ball came out of his hand like it had been whipped somehow, building velocity as it approached and then dropping suddenly as it crossed the plate. The batter made a stab at it with his bat, and missed it totally. *SLAP!*

"Seventy-five," called out Uncle Rob.

The first guy was gone in three pitches. The following guys could barely make contact with the ball. It was basically strike out, strike out, strike out. Kyle's old teammates were laughing and shaking their heads. "I still can't hit you, bro!" yelled one guy, tossing his batting helmet into the dead grass.

After a half hour of this, I wandered over to where Uncle Rob was standing with his radar gun. Without looking at me, he said: "You wanna take a few swings?"

I laughed. I assumed he was kidding. But he wasn't.

I didn't know what to say. I didn't really want to. It looked terrifying out there.

Some of the other players standing nearby had heard Uncle Rob's offer. They kind of smiled but then looked away, so as not to embarrass me. They understood my hesitation. They were baseball guys, they were used to good pitchers. I was just some guy.

On the other hand, I didn't want to look like a wuss. I

was a decent athlete. There was no reason I couldn't try to bat against my cousin.

"Okay," I said.

Uncle Rob looked surprised. So did the other guys. But they approved. They immediately began to encourage me. Someone found me a batting helmet and a special pad to put over my elbow, in case I got hit. They told me what to do. Where to stand. They applauded my bravery, or my stupidity, it was hard to tell. Anyway, a minute later, in my $9.99 sneakers and Happy Bubble shirt, I walked around the backstop.

Oh God, I thought as I approached home plate. There was a lot of empty space out there. And not having the fence between me and those sizzling baseballs made my knees go weak.

I had no choice now. I'd said I'd do it and here I was. I stood at the plate. I took a couple practice swings. The bat was small, so that was good. I took a couple more practice swings.

Kyle, meanwhile, looked skeptical. He stepped off the rubber and gave his dad a look like, *What are you doing?* When his dad just shrugged, he looked at me like, *Are you sure you want to do this?*

I nodded that I did. I stood in, taking more nervous practice swings.

Kyle took his stance. He looked into his mitt and gripped the baseball. A queasy liquid feeling immediately spread from the top of my neck down into my stomach.

Kyle went into his windup. I could feel my feet trying to back me out of there. My whole body wanted to dive for cover. Kyle completed his motion and suddenly the ball was in the air, there was a hissing sound, and then *SLAP!* The ball was past me before I could think, before I could move.

I stepped away, my whole body quivering. Holy *shit.*

"Seventy-one," announced Uncle Rob.

I tried to calm myself. I tried swinging the bat again. But my arms had become rubbery and my hands felt numb and detached from the rest of my body. Fear: it could really mess you up.

"Nick!" yelled a voice from behind me. Was that *Emily?* I turned and saw her pressed against the backstop.

Beside her was Jace. "Are you out of your frickin' mind?!" yelled Jace.

Great. That's all I needed. I turned back toward Kyle and then spotted Mike, from the Happy Bubble, standing off to the side. The whole town was here suddenly. How had this happened?

I refocused on Kyle. I stepped back up to the plate. He waited until I was ready, then went into his slow, deliberate windup again. It was kind of fascinating to watch. Each separate movement had been practiced and perfected. A flawless motion, at the end of which a deadly round ball, hard as a rock, came sizzling at your face, missing you by inches.

This time I could actually follow the ball for a fleeting

second before it passed me. *SLAP!* The bat never left my shoulder. "Seventy-four," said Uncle Rob. "Throw him a curve."

I didn't know what that was going to look like. But I prepared myself. I was, for a moment, aware of Jace's presence. I was glad she was seeing this.

Kyle wound up again. I gritted my teeth and focused with every fiber of my being. With a tiny hesitation, the pitch appeared from a slightly different place on his body. It came straight for a moment and then, with astonishing movement, curved away from me. I had planned to swing no matter what, and I did, but the ball looped away from me so far and so fast that I lurched forward, tripped over home plate, and ended up in the dirt, nearly hitting myself in the forehead with the bat.

"Sixty-four," said Uncle Rob. Everyone else was laughing. Only Kyle ran forward when he saw my awkward fall, face-first into the ground.

"You okay?" he asked, helping me up.

"Yeah, yeah," I said, dusting myself off.

"Nice try!" yelled one of the guys.

"Way to go, Nick," said someone else.

Several people clapped.

"Oh my God!" I heard Jace say, behind me. "You almost killed yourself!"

11

That night, after work, Emily texted that she and Jace and Kelsey were going to the Sandpiper. Did I want to meet them?

I said yes. It would give me an excuse to avoid Justin. The girls were already in a booth when I got there. I squeezed in and ordered a milk shake when the waitress came. They were talking about different boys and other goings-on in their social world. There was a party later up in Astoria, which was thirty-five miles to the north. I could tell by how they talked that they considered Astoria to be just up the road, a nearby neighborhood. I was learning that's how people thought about distances on the coast. Thirty-five miles was nothing, especially if there was a party.

"Nick came home totally drunk last night," Emily suddenly announced to the table.

All three girls turned toward me.

"*You* got drunk?" said Jace. "*Responsible Nick?* How did that happen?"

"He was with Justin," said Emily. "From the car wash."

"Ha-ha," said Jace. "Well, that explains it."

"Wait," I said. "Did you just call me *Responsible Nick?*"

"He was crashing around," continued Emily. "Trying to get in the basement door. I was like, *Uh-oh. . . .*"

The girls all laughed.

"Hold on," I said. "*Responsible Nick?* Is that what I'm known as?" I was sort of kidding, but sort of not.

"*No!* Not at all!" said Jace, with sarcastic concern. "We don't call you that. We don't call people things."

"It's not an insult; it's a compliment," said Emily.

"So you *do* call me that," I said.

The girls all looked at Emily. "Don't look at me," she said. "I didn't start it."

"You did too start it," said Jace.

"No," said Emily. "As I recall, *you* started it, Jace."

"Or maybe Kelsey started it."

"I didn't start it!" said Kelsey.

I interrupted: "Can I just ask *why* you call me that?"

"Because," said Jace. "You're so responsible."

"You want everyone to get home safe," said Emily.

"Like the night at the movies," said Jace. "You were so worried about Kelsey and Lauren."

"You were *more* worried about Carson and Wyatt," said Emily.

"But I didn't know them!" I protested.

The girls looked at each other. "Well," said Jace. "That's why you're Responsible Nick."

"You like to check up on people," said Emily.

"You're very concerned!" laughed Jace.

They were totally teasing me now. I got it. I laughed. It was sort of funny. But seriously, who wants to be known as *Responsible Nick*?

Later, we went to the party in Astoria. Tonight Jace was driving. She was sixteen, it turned out, and in the same grade as me, and also sort of smart, according to what she said about her classes.

The party was in the woods, on top of a hill. We parked along a road and walked uphill to a clearing where people were standing around a keg.

We each paid our five bucks for a plastic cup and lined up to fill them with foamy beer. Then we stood around with the other people. Astorians were similar to Seasiders, I noticed. Guys with trucker hats, flannels, baggy jeans. Girls with the strange choppy hairstyles you only saw on the coast. There was weed and pipes and lighters. People took deep hits and then cocked their heads back to blow long streams of smoke into the cold night sky.

A bit later a different boy showed up and came over to Emily. His name was Oliver. He was better dressed than the others and better looking. He and Emily walked off somewhere. Then Jace and Kelsey began whispering to each other about something. This left me to hang with the Astoria guys, who were talking about Tasers.

"Dude, my cousin got tased. He said you can't do nothin'. You can't think, you can't move . . ."

"And you're all jerkin' around and shit. . . ."

"I heard you piss yourself."

"I know this guy said he just pulled the thing off. Like before they could zap him."

"You can't pull it out. The minute it hits you, you're zapped."

"I saw them tase this guy at Burger King once . . . some homeless dude. . . ."

"I heard it can kill you. If they keep doin' it? You can't breathe. Cuz your muscles are all seized up."

"Nah, you don't die—that's the whole point. . . ."

"You can buy 'em online. Tasers. Four hundred bucks. You could tase yourself."

"Now why would you want to tase yourself?"

"You could tase a dog, I guess. . . ."

"Or someone comes at you. You could tase 'em."

"Someone breaks into your house . . ."

The conversation went on like that. Eventually I went back to Jace and Kelsey. Emily and Oliver were still off doing whatever in the woods.

And then a police siren squawked from the road below. Through the trees I could make out the rotating lights of a slow-moving cop car. I quickly looked around for an escape route, assuming the Astoria people would make a run for it, into the forest. That's what we did in Eugene when the police showed up.

But nobody seemed concerned.

"Here comes Tony," said someone.

"Tony's here!"

"Tony the cop."

People casually refilled their beers and drank them down a little faster than before. When the siren squawked again, they finished their cups and tossed them into a brown paper bag someone had thoughtfully provided. They gathered their stuff and began to amble down the trail toward their cars. Jace and Kelsey and I followed the others.

Down below, the cop car was stopped in the middle of the road, its lights flashing.

"Hey, Tony!" someone called.

"Tony! Wudup?"

"Tony the cop!"

The squad car was a modified Mustang with cop lights on it and ASTORIA POLICE painted on the side. When we got closer, I looked in the passenger window. The guy driving the car, Tony, looked like a real cop, young but with an official uniform. But the guy sitting in the passenger side was just some dude with a mustache and a dorky expression on his face. Tony was talking to some people on his side of the car. He asked what kind of beer we were drinking. When someone said Pabst, he said, "Pabst? That piss water? I wouldn't drink that shit if you paid me!" The kids all laughed. It was pretty funny how casual everybody was.

Tony remained in the middle of the road until most of the partiers had left. Then he left too. We were still there, standing beside our car, waiting for Emily, who had not returned from the woods with Oliver.

Finally, they appeared on the trail above us. Oliver was touching Emily's shoulder, like he was trying to convince her of something. Emily was not being convinced. Then he turned her toward him and kissed her. She did not resist this, I noticed. Jace saw that I was watching them and laughed.

"Don't worry, Nick," she said to me. "Everything's fine. Everyone's okay."

Driving home, I felt annoyed with Jace. I wasn't that worried about Emily. I wasn't that uptight about people. And I did not want to be referred to as *Responsible Nick* for the rest of the summer, that's for sure. What if my friends in Eugene found out people were calling me that?

My ex-girlfriend Kate, she was the responsible one. I remembered the first time I saw her in English class, sophomore year. You could *feel* how organized she was. Her tight hair bun. Her clothes all matched. Even her posture was perfect. And naturally, she was super smart in that class.

I was more the smart-ass guy in the back. Or I was at the start of the year. Once my mom got arrested again, I stopped being so quick with the witty comments.

The problem was, all this stuff I didn't know started coming out. My mother didn't just have an alcohol problem. She had boyfriends. She did cocaine. She lied and had mood swings and rammed her car into the mailboxes of people she didn't like. She had two DUIs and couldn't legally drive in California. My dad had to sit me down and explain it all to me.

Needless to say, this messed with my head in a big way. I felt like *I* was the one in trouble. And my mother, who had always been difficult to deal with, now became impossible. I went into advanced avoidance mode, slipping in and out of the house as quick as I could. School was better, but not by much. There was no actual enjoying things or pursuing something . . . like a girlfriend. I couldn't trust myself in social situations. I'd be standing around with my buddies, and some bizarre thing would pop out of my mouth. Or I'd start babbling or get pissed off for no reason. I just wasn't right in the head.

But then, in all that confusion, there was Kate. I'd see her in the hallways, or in our English class, and I'd feel better instantly. She was so *solid*. And she was cute and a girl and soft and all that. Whatever it was, she made me feel better. Just *knowing* she'd be in English class, fourth period, third desk from the window: It got me through the day.

When I noticed she sometimes went to the library after school, I started going there too. I didn't expect anything to happen. We weren't really friends. But then, the first time she saw me there, she walked right up and started telling me something about our homework. It wasn't flirty or romantic, which made it easy to respond. It was like an instant calm came over me. I felt like my old self again.

That was November of sophomore year. So then after we'd talked a couple times, we made up some reason to meet at the Springdale Mall. We never said it was a date, but we both knew it was. We met up and got smoothies and walked around. She was a little nervous, and so was I, but it was a good nervous, a comfortable nervous. It was easy being with her. I felt like I didn't need to tell her about my mother, not right away, and that when I did, it would be okay. I actually thought she might know already, since that was starting to happen.

We walked around for a couple hours, and then I kissed her, waiting in the bus shelter outside. It was cold and raining, but that made it better in a way. We kissed for a few minutes and then held each other and kept each other warm. I smoothed Kate's hair with my hand for some reason, like she was the hurt one, though she didn't seem to be hurt at all. She was the definition of unhurt. Her family was super normal. Which was a relief.

Soon after, Kate and I had "the conversation." Dr. Snow had coached me on what to say. We were sitting on the bench outside the library. It was after school; nobody was around. I told Kate my mother had a drinking problem.

She looked surprised when I said this. She didn't know

anything about it. "Like what kind of drinking problem?" she said.

"She drinks too much, and she gets in trouble."

"In trouble? Like how?"

"Like drunk driving. And other things."

"But she's a *professor*. . . ."

"Yeah, I know."

Kate thought about this. "Well why doesn't she . . . can't she just not drink so much?"

"She tries. We all try to help her. But certain people get addicted to alcohol, and they can't stop."

"So she's an *alcoholic* . . . ," said Kate. I remember the look on her face. Like in her mind she was trying to figure out what this meant and how it would affect the two of us. "But aren't there places for people like that? Rehabs?"

"Yeah, she went to one. And it worked for a while. But then she started again. She's going to go back. That's the plan."

Kate nodded. She looked sad now, and upset.

"I know," I said. "It's super frustrating."

Kate was still having trouble believing all this. She really liked my mom. And she respected that she was a professor. Kate had actually read my mother's book, *The Gender Response*, and got it autographed by her.

"I wasn't sure when exactly to tell you," I said, looking into Kate's lap.

"So she drinks like . . . all the time?"

"Not all the time," I said.

"I'm sorry," said Kate, getting frustrated again. "But I find it hard to believe that a *college professor* . . . an *author* . . . it just doesn't seem *possible*."

"I know. But it's true. I thought I needed to tell you. So I'm telling you."

"That's so weird," she said.

"I know."

She looked into the distance. "I don't know what to say."

"You don't have to say anything."

After that first conversation we didn't talk about it again. Not until the night my dad punched Richard in the face, in our front yard, and the cops came and my dad got hauled off to jail. After that everyone was talking about it. That was the period when I sometimes slept in the basement at Kate's. Of course I'd creep upstairs and sleep in Kate's bed with her for part of the night, and then sneak back down before her parents woke up. The sad thing was we never had sex. That was Kate's one negative reaction to the situation. She became reluctant to do certain things. Most couples our age, if they loved each other, and were together for a while, they had sex. But we never did, which was messed up. Kate should have been my first. She was my first love. The first person I told everything to. The first person I trusted completely. Kate not being my first, that was the worst thing of all.

13

During the last weekend of June summer finally arrived in Seaside. Eighty-six degrees, with clear bright skies. This was great for business, but not the best time to be wearing a 100% polyester uniform shirt, which was hot and scratchy. Long black Dickies were also not the most comfortable choice. Fortunately, even when it was hot, there was still the ocean breeze, which always kept things tolerable.

We got swamped with customers. The line of cars went out to the highway. The tunnel was turned up to max speed, and Justin and I scrambled to keep up with the windexing and vacuuming. It was fun in a way, racing around, rushing to finish each car. Kyle was in charge in the morning, and then Uncle Rob came in and took over. When it got really busy, he even helped us, cleaning windows in his unique side-to-side style.

At one point Nicole and Phoebe came in to talk to Kyle. They only stayed a minute, but then later Kyle pulled me aside and told me there was a big beach party happening that night and did I want to do a beer run with him? Of course I did. I then texted Emily and Jace to tell them about the party. Emily wrote back: *We already know.*

I was psyched, though. *A beach party!* This was one of the main things I'd looked forward to, coming to Seaside: beach fires, people playing guitars, pretty girls with blankets around their shoulders and their bare toes curled in the sand.

We closed the Happy Bubble at eight. Then Kyle and I drove north of town to a large store called Billy Malone's Beer and Spirits. Kyle parked in the gravel parking lot in back and strode inside, with me hurrying along beside him.

It was a big deal when Kyle Reilly stepped inside Billy Malone's. Everyone wanted to say hi. There were lots of questions about his baseball workouts. How was his arm holding up? How did the team look? Would they win another Pac-12 championship next year? Kyle handled it perfectly as always. He was always humble, always polite. Then Billy himself—the old guy who owned the place— took us into the large refrigerated stockroom. Kyle pointed out six cases of cheap American beer. Without a word, two of Billy's guys quickly loaded them into Uncle Rob's truck. Even these guys were in awe of Kyle, I noticed, glancing up at him, moving extra fast since it was him.

This was totally illegal, since Kyle was only eighteen. I

don't know how he paid for it. Maybe he had a tab. Maybe Uncle Rob had a tab. When we were all loaded up, Kyle thanked Billy and shook his hand.

"Good luck, Kyle," said the old man, his eyes sparkling, both of his hands still gripping Kyle's. "We're all pulling for you. A young man, like yourself. You make us very proud. You know that, don't you?"

"I do," said Kyle. "And I appreciate it. Thanks, Billy."

Back in the truck Kyle pulled up to the highway and waited for the traffic to clear. I said, "You really know how to handle that stuff."

"What stuff?" he said.

"You know, people wanting to congratulate you. People wanting a piece of you."

"They don't want a piece of me. They're just happy for me. That's all."

"But isn't it a lot of pressure? On you?"

Kyle shrugged in his casual way. "It doesn't feel like pressure."

"Well, you're lucky then."

Kyle thought about it for a moment. "It's just what you gotta do," he said. "People give you love. You give it back. What else you gonna do?"

I nodded at that.

A break came in the traffic. Kyle hit the gas, and we rumbled onto the highway.

"And anyway," he said as the cab filled with rushing air. "It could all end tomorrow. I could get hurt. I could blow out my arm. Gotta enjoy it while ya got it."

He looked at me and grinned. I grinned back. He hung his elbow out the open window. "I'm glad you're here this summer," he said. "I know we can't hang too much. But it's nice."

"Yeah," I said. "It is."

Back home Kyle and I microwaved some meat loaf for dinner. I took a shower and went downstairs to get dressed. *My first beach party*, I thought. I put on some Old Spice and brushed my hair. It would be cold at the beach at night, even after a hot day, so I wore my wool sweater. I also stuck *Letters to a Young Poet* in my back pocket, in case there was someone at the party who might appreciate something like that. It wasn't likely, but if there was, it would give us something to talk about.

I went back upstairs and sat outside on the front porch while I waited for Kyle. As I stared down the hill at the trees and the road, it occurred to me how far away I was from my old life. I hadn't talked to my dad for a week. I hadn't talked to my mom since I left Eugene. There'd been no sessions with Dr. Snow.

I was really on my own now, and it felt good. And now I had a beach party to go to.

Kyle and I drove south on the highway to the last stoplight in Seaside. We turned right toward the ocean and followed an asphalt road, traversing the side of Tillamook Head, which was a huge mountain that stuck out into the sea. We drove along that, beside the ocean, looking down through the trees at the surf.

At the end of the road was a gravel parking area on a bluff. Kyle parked and we got out. I walked to the edge, and there, down below us, was a beautiful crescent beach with several driftwood-fire sites. This was the Cove, which I'd heard Justin and other people talk about. This was Seaside's famous party spot.

A few people were down there already, standing around in shorts and T-shirts, others carrying firewood. Another car pulled in. These people greeted Kyle and chatted with him as they gathered their blankets and wine bottles and back-packs. I watched as they began the somewhat treacherous descent down the trail. They were older, in their twenties, with thick hairy legs and facial stubble. "See you!" they called to Kyle as they disappeared down the hill.

As more people arrived, Kyle recruited some helpers to carry our beer to the beach. It wasn't easy carrying a thirty-pack along that trail. I nearly toppled over when I tripped on an exposed root.

On the beach Kyle told me he had to pick someone up and climbed back up the trail by himself. This was probably Britney, his current and supposedly doomed girlfriend. So I was left with a bunch of older people I didn't know, who were building the fire. I helped gather driftwood with them, then helped blow on the fledgling flames, then helped cele-brate when it finally got going by helping myself to a beer.

It was nine thirty when the sun touched the horizon that night. By then there were about thirty people on the beach and more coming down the trail. I didn't know most of them, but then Justin appeared. I was glad to see a familiar face. He was dressed in jeans and a Western shirt, and of course he had a joint, which he fired up the second his foot hit the sand. He was with one of his stoner buddies, Tyler, who had thick black hair and weird fang teeth.

Then I saw Jace coming down the hill. I was even more excited to see her. She was wearing skinny jeans and a pon-cho. Emily was next, in Bermuda shorts and a sweater, and

Kelsey was behind her, in a hoodie. They would be the youngest people at the party, by quite a lot, but I noticed that people seemed excited to see them. I remembered that Emily was Kyle's little sister, which probably made her an important person in the Seaside world. This explained certain things, like why she was so sure of herself.

When Jace and Emily got down the hill, they didn't come over to me, though they obviously saw me. I guess they were being cool. Whatever. It was fine. Everything seemed perfect just as it was. I stayed with Justin and Tyler, drinking beer and taking hits off their joint. The sun was now down, which lit up the sky, bright pink and red to the west, while to the east the dark blue of night was gathering above the mountaintops. I stood, holding my beer against my stomach, and listened to the party talk and the crackling fire. Cars were still pulling up in the parking lot. You'd hear the different music from each car stereo, and you could guess what type of people they would be when they appeared on the trail. It was quite a scene there at the Cove. Everyone was laughing and smiling and having a great time. The mood was like: *Finally, it's summer!*

Emily, Jace, and Kelsey had a blanket, I noticed, and had neatly spread it out a proper distance from the fire. I checked on them occasionally, waiting for a good moment to go over there. Eventually, Jace caught my eye and waved me over.

"How's it going, Responsible Nick?" she teased.

"It's going all right," I said, sitting down on the edge of their blanket. I somehow lost my balance and fell over sideways in the sand. The girls all gawked at me.

"What?" I said, righting myself. "I'm not used to sitting in sand."

"How hard is it to sit in sand?" said Emily.

Jace was more welcoming. "Look at you, all dressed up in your nice sweater!" she said.

"Thanks," I said. I got my butt properly settled and took a swig of my beer. Jace sat beside me. An older guy appeared and began chatting up Emily and Kelsey. He was holding his longneck beer bottle in that way older dudes did, using it as a pointer and being very suave and cool. Emily listened to him for a few seconds, then ignored him.

"This is my first beach party," I told Jace.

"Really? Ever in your life?"

"Ever in my life," I said. "I keep waiting for someone to get a guitar out. That's what they do in beer commercials."

"Is that how you define things, by beer commercials?" she said, smiling.

"I guess so. How else would I define them?"

"But commercials show you a fake version. Since they're trying to sell you something."

"Well, at least it's *a* version," I said. "At least it gives you the basic idea."

Jace thought about that. We both sat for a moment, staring at the fire.

"How's the Happy Bubble?" she asked.

"Good," I said. "Lots of customers today. With the heat."

"What do you do there?"

"I vacuum mostly. Me and Justin. And clean windows." I took a sip of my beer. "Yeah. Mostly we vacuum up small change. Out of the ashtray, out of the carpets. And then we split it at the end of shift."

"How much do you usually get?"

"Five or ten bucks."

"I'll keep that in mind next time I get my car washed. Hide your change."

"Oh, you can't hide it. We'll find it. We're professionals." Jace laughed. "I bet!"

"What about you?" I said. "Do you have a job?"

"I work at the library," said Jace.

"Really?" I said, pulling my beer away from my mouth. "There's a library here? Where is it?"

"It's behind the Dunes Hotel. It's small. The hours are a little weird. But I'm usually there."

"I'll come check it out."

"Are you a reader?" she asked.

"Yeah. I mean, sometimes." I dug around in my back pocket and pulled out Rilke's *Letters to a Young Poet*. "I've been trying to read this. It's my summer reading for AP English. But I haven't gotten very far."

Jace took the book from me and studied the cover. "I don't know this."

"It's this German guy. A poet. It's his words of advice for young writers."

"Do you want to be a writer?"

"Me? *Nah.* I don't know. Maybe. My mom wrote a book."

"Yeah? What's it about?"

"I don't know. *Gender.* It's hard to read. It's for academic types."

"Sounds deep."

"Yeah," I said, taking Rilke's *Letters* back. "My English teacher suggested this. It's short, so that's good. But I can't seem to get into it."

"I know," said Jace. "I totally do that. I save certain books for the summer, but then when summer comes, I can't read them. I just want to read something stupid. Romance novels. Or something with lots of sex."

"Yeah," I said. "I like stuff with sex."

She suddenly saw something over my head. "Oh, look! Kyle's here. With his girlfriend."

I looked up the trail, and there they were. Kyle, looking clean and collegiate, and a girl I'd never seen before, also well-dressed, in Levi's and a baby-blue down vest.

"That's Britney?" I asked Jace.

"That's her."

"She's kind of doomed, isn't she," I said.

"How do you mean?"

"Just that Kyle's going to leave for college."

"That doesn't mean she's *doomed.*"

"Well, no," I said. "I guess not."

People began to see Kyle and Britney and yell out greetings.

"Everyone's always happy to see Kyle," said Jace. She leaned a little closer. "But the party doesn't *really* start until Nicole gets here."

Nicole and Phoebe showed up a half hour later. Nicole started yelling and waving from the parking lot. While everyone watched her shriek and stumble down the trail, my eye followed Phoebe, who was behind her. Phoebe was wearing tight black jeans and red sneakers, and was having less trouble than Nicole, carefully stepping over the roots and avoiding the slippery spots.

As they descended, I wondered what was going on with Kyle and Britney and Nicole. Was everyone cool with everyone else? Nicole was obviously still in love with Kyle and wasn't shy about it. What did Britney think about that?

Once it got dark, Justin came over and plopped himself down next to Jace and me. He got out another joint. The party had spread up and down the beach by this time. There were several other fires burning. Some of these groups were separate from us but I noticed people were circulating around, blending together, sharing wine or weed or marshmallows. Four brave tourists—two guys, two girls—had stripped down to their underwear, run down the beach, and dove into the freezing ocean. Now they huddled close to our fire, blankets over their shoulders, warming their shivering selves. Beside them some local guys were trying to cook hot dogs on sticks, while some traveling surfer dudes discussed the morning's waves. Then two soft-spoken Norwegian guys sat down and told us about their bike-riding trip across the United States, which they were about to begin, Seaside being the traditional starting point for such trips. This explained why you'd sometimes see gangs of foreigners clustered around the Promenade in expensive biking gear. Anyway, there was all sorts of fun stuff going on and interesting people to talk to. And of course, sitting together in the firelight, everyone was happy and in a good mood, sipping their beers and enjoying that cozy, communal, beach-party feeling.

Emily and Kelsey went off somewhere, and then Jace and I went for a walk on the beach. We talked about high school and life in general. She wanted to go to college, but her school counselor mostly sent people to community college or maybe Oregon State if they wanted to study forestry or agriculture. Jace's parents hadn't gone to college, so they weren't much help either. Jace herself didn't seem to know which schools were good and which ones weren't. I tried to explain about that, how you didn't judge schools by their campus, or if they were in a sunny climate. It was more about what kind of people went there, and what the academic reputation was. I told her about my mom, how she had gone to a small women's college in Minnesota and then transferred to University of Wisconsin, which had better professors. Then she went to Berkeley for grad school, and finally to Yale for her PhD. With every step, she had moved up in terms of prestige and reputation. The better the schools you went to, the better the jobs you got. That was how the academic world worked.

This was probably more information than Jace needed, but I thought it would help. I also told her it was good she was from Seaside. The top colleges liked people from unusual places. Especially somewhere like Seaside, which was so working class. She could write her college essay about her life there and the lessons she learned from working people. It would help her stand out from the other college applicants, who were mostly rich kids who lived in the suburbs.

It was later, when we were back on our blanket, that the drama started with Nicole. I didn't see it; I just heard Nicole's loud, drunken voice arguing with someone, not Kyle. Someone else was telling her to calm down, but she wouldn't. And then she went storming down the beach, making sure she marched right through the people around our fire, kicking up sand and knocking people's beers over.

I didn't know where Britney was, or Kyle, probably somewhere else on the beach. Nobody seemed to think much of it. Later Nicole came back to our fire and sat on a log and drank wine from a bottle, while the guy next to her tried to look down her shirt. Phoebe was also around, beer in hand and looking sexy and bored in the firelight. Different guys were hitting on her, chatting her up, trying to impress her. She barely said anything back, I noticed. I thought if I ever got a chance to talk to Phoebe, I'd ask her questions, because a girl like that might have something interesting to say. Why would you just babble at her about your stupid motorcycle? Probably every guy in Seaside had tried that a hundred times.

At one a.m., Emily and Jace and those guys had to go home. I decided I better go with them, since I wasn't sure where Kyle was, or what he was doing. The bunch of us climbed up the trail. It had been a great night, for me especially, and when we reached the parking lot, I stopped and looked down one last time. It looked so peaceful down on the beach. The soft sounds of voices and laughter rising up from the sand. The firelight on the people's faces. The stars shining and the cool night air that smelled like summer dust and pine trees. And beyond all that, the big black ocean, vast and calm, like a great mysterious being, watching us, protecting us, loving us from afar.

Driving home, everyone talked about the party, except for Emily, who stared out the window. When Kelsey tried to gossip about Kyle and Nicole, Emily said, "I'd rather not talk about my brother." So then the car went quiet for the rest of the ride.

Jace dropped Kelsey off first and then drove to the Reillys'. The minute we pulled up, Emily jumped out of the back seat and ran up the driveway toward the house. I was in the front passenger seat and was getting out too, but Jace touched my arm, holding me until Emily was gone.

"Hey, that was fun," she said.

"That was great," I said. "My first beach party!"

"Was it better than a beer commercial?"

"Way better."

Jace smiled in a bashful way. "And thanks for explaining that stuff about colleges."

"No problem," I said. "I only know about it because of my mom."

"Well, it's good for me. I don't know anything."

"Yeah," I said. "It's pretty important . . . what college you go to . . . it can affect your whole life. . . ."

Jace was looking at me a certain way. I didn't understand at first. Then she unhooked her seat belt and leaned toward me. She kissed me. On the lips.

I wasn't expecting that. I didn't react. Then I recovered, sort of, kissing her back for a second. But inside, I was like, *What does this mean?* Did I like Jace? I mean, I *did* like her. I liked hanging out with her. I liked talking to her. But I hadn't thought of her as a person I would make out with.

I guess she sensed this, because she pulled away and returned to her own seat.

"Anyway, thanks," she said. She seemed flustered now. She wouldn't meet my eye. She refastened her seat belt. Then I felt bad. I wanted to say something. Or maybe kiss her some more. But the moment had passed. And I was embarrassed too. So I opened my door and thanked her again and hurried up the driveway.

Back in my room, I sat on my bed. I couldn't believe
Jace had kissed me. Seaside girls didn't mess around! Then
I remembered Emily asking me if I had a girlfriend back
home. And asking me if I liked tall girls. So maybe this was
something the two of them had been planning all along.

I took off my jeans and sweater and brushed the sand out
of them. I could hear through the ceiling Emily going into
the bathroom and the toilet flushing and her going back to
her room. So then I went upstairs and brushed my teeth
and looked at myself in the mirror. I thought about Jace. I
almost wanted to go talk to Emily about her but decided I
better not. I went back downstairs to my basement room.
It was two a.m. now. I got in bed. But I was too excited to
sleep. I thought about the party. I thought about the entire
night. And then the most important question: *Could I like*

Jace? I pictured her face. She wasn't super beautiful. But that didn't matter. She was like Kate, cute in a way, but the real appeal was she was someone you felt comfortable with, someone you could care about and who would care about you. It was funny that she called me Responsible Nick. I guess I seemed that way by Seaside standards. As for the kiss, the more I thought about it, the more I wished I'd kept it going.

I fell asleep for a couple hours and then woke up again. I lay in the dark and thought about other things: School. My mom. *College.* How, when I got back to Eugene, I would need to kick ass for that first semester of senior year, and then really focus on my college applications. I couldn't get distracted. It was tricky, though, because one of the best assets I had was my mother. She had connections. She was famous in her field. I would need to use that somehow, but also not let her screw me up. She was like that. Sometimes she'd help you. Sometimes she wouldn't. You never knew for sure.

Thinking about that made me anxious, and then I really couldn't sleep. I decided to read some of *Letters to a Young Poet*. I grabbed my pants off the floor and looked for it, but it wasn't in my back pocket. Where was it? I'd shown it to Jace while we were sitting on the blanket. Had she not given it back? Maybe someone else had looked at it. Or maybe it fell out of my pocket. I searched the entire basement floor and under the bed. It was not there.

Oh great, I thought, flopping back onto the bed. The one book I actually needed to read this summer, and I'd lost it. And it was a library book! I'd have to get another copy somehow. I pulled the covers over me, but now I was totally awake. I could see through the window that it was already getting light outside. I checked my phone. It was 5:23 a.m. Jesus. Could I go back to the beach somehow? That's probably where it was.

I rolled off my bed and got dressed. I quietly opened the basement door and checked the driveway. Uncle Rob's pickup was there; Kyle had brought it home. Nobody would be awake for several hours. I knew where the extra set of keys was—Uncle Rob had showed me, in case I needed the car for some reason. Those were his exact words: "for some reason." Could I drive it down to the Cove really quick and get my book? I didn't see why not.

I got the keys and took the truck. I was super careful. I pulled backward onto the road and then shifted to DRIVE and slowly made my way to the highway. The truck was easy to drive, especially with no other cars on the road. I followed the route Kyle had taken. Down the hill, south through town, and then taking a right at the last stoplight. It was kinda fun to be out at that hour, with no cars, no humans, no movement. I followed the road along Tillamook Head. The ocean, I noticed, was smooth, calm, a beautiful aqua green.

I pulled into the parking lot above the Cove. It had

taken me twelve minutes to get there. I went to the edge and looked down. There was a lot of crap on the beach. Empty bottles. Plastic cups. A broken beach chair. An abandoned sleeping bag. Two of the fires were still smoking slightly.

I made my way down the trail. The ocean was much closer to our bonfire than it had been the night before. It must have been high tide.

I walked through the sand to our fire site. The beach looked strange and different in the morning light. Still, I felt like I could calculate where Jace's blanket had been. I stood in that spot and looked around. When I didn't see my book, I began to comb the sand with my fingers, in case it got buried somehow. But I didn't find it. So then I began to walk around the fire. Did someone else pick it up? I walked around the logs where people had been sitting. There was one really big log; I looked under it. Something smooth and square was half buried beneath it. I looked closer. It was my book! I reached under and grabbed it and wiped the sand away. It was a little damp, a little wrinkly, but otherwise okay. *Thank God,* I thought. I stood up and crammed it into my back pocket.

So that was a relief. I looked out at the ocean, then at the beach. There was a lot of trash around: cigarette butts, a watermelon rind, empty beer cans, wine bottles. I wondered if I should clean up a little. It could be my good deed for the day, and it was so peaceful and nice there, I didn't want to leave just yet. I would need a large garbage bag, though, or some sort of container. I looked on the other side of the big log and saw a tattered old sleeping bag. Maybe I could put the garbage in that and then dump the whole mess in the trash can at the top of the trail. I leaned over the log to grab the sleeping bag but stopped short. There was something under it. There was *a person* under it.

I jumped backward. I looked around the beach, which was totally deserted. Who would still be down here? And why? I inched forward, looking at the sleeping bag again. There was definitely a human-sized *thing* underneath it. I moved down the log a few feet, crawled over and approached the sleeping bag from the other side. I crouched down beside it and carefully gripped the top. I gently pulled it back.

The first thing I saw was hair. Black hair. It was a girl's hair, but matted and wet, with sand in it and debris, and beneath it the very white skin of someone's scalp. I pulled it back more. I saw an ear, a neck, the side of a face. And then I recognized the person.

It was *Phoebe*.

I pulled the sleeping bag down more. There she was.
Phoebe. Curled on her side. In one way I was horrified. In
another way I was thrilled. I touched her shoulder. She was
warm. So she wasn't dead.

But she wasn't exactly alive, either. She was so still,
so completely asleep. Or was she passed out? Jesus, what
was wrong with people? Who left her here? And how
drunk must she have been. Were people in Seaside *totally
insane?*

I bent down and put my face near her mouth. She was
breathing. That was good. My next thought was to get her
off the cold sand. I would need to wake her up, though.

"Phoebe?" I said. "Hello?" I tried nudging her. Gently
at first and then harder. When that didn't work, I eased her
onto her back. Then I got behind her and gripped her by the

armpits and lifted her to a sitting position. I tried to keep the sleeping bag around her. She had her clothes on, thank God. I propped her up, my hands around her from behind. I brushed the sand off her, and then tried shaking her and squeezing her shoulders.

She began to make noises. Her head, which had been hanging forward, moved slightly.

"Uhhhhhhh . . . ," she said.

"Phoebe? Hello? Are you okay?"

Her head rolled to one side. But then it lifted. Suddenly she was awake. She began to look around.

"Do you know where you are?" I said. I was on my knees, behind her, holding her up. When she realized there was a person there, gripping her, she pushed away from me, and then glared back at me with a vague, hostile look. Her eyes weren't really focusing. "I'm Nick," I said. "Remember? I work at the car wash. With Kyle."

She didn't seem to hear me. She was coming more fully to life. With unexpected energy she shrugged off the sleeping bag and struggled to her feet. I moved back and got to my feet as well. As the sleeping bag fell away, I saw that her pants were undone. She was covered with sand, and her clothes were damp and wet. Her face was ghostly pale, and her hair was a tangled mess.

"Jesus," I said. "You don't look too good."

She didn't answer.

"How did you get left here?" I asked.

She didn't answer that, either. She glanced around the

beach, squinting and looking pained. She must have had a brutal hangover.

"I have my uncle's truck," I said. "I can give you a ride."

She didn't respond. She wasn't really seeing me, I realized. She was surveying the beach, doing a primitive calculation of what to do next. She decided to climb the hill and began walking through the sand to the trail. I followed along behind her. Again, she surprised me with her energy. She scrambled right up the steep hill, no problem. I stayed with her. In the parking lot, in her confusion, she turned back to me.

"Do you need a ride?" I offered. "Here. Here's my truck."

I walked her to the passenger side, opened the door, and helped her in.

I hurried around and got in the driver's side. I started the truck and told her to put on her seat belt, which she did. She seemed to be physically functional. And yet she still said nothing.

I cranked the heat and drove fast along the asphalt road back to Seaside. At the stoplight, I turned left onto the highway toward town. Phoebe was staring blankly out the front windshield as I did this. She began smoothing her hair and picking the stuff out of it, dropping the twigs and bits of moss onto the floor.

I tried again to communicate with her. "Seriously . . . ," I said. "Are you okay? Do you want me to take you to the hospital?"

She didn't answer.

"Where can I take you?" I said.

She said nothing for another minute but then started to point. I drove where she pointed. We ended up on one of the residential streets on the north side of town. She pointed to a small house, and I pulled up in front. "Phoebe," I said, thinking maybe her name would return her to reality. "Phoebe, please. Can you at least tell me you're okay? I can't tell if you are. I don't even know if this is your house."

But I hardly got the words out before she sprung her seat belt and was out of the truck, running up the driveway of the small, modest home. I wished I'd driven slower, so I could have had a little more time with her. She disappeared inside, and I sat there for a moment, staring at the front door, trying to fully digest the last fifteen minutes.

What on earth had just happened? I had no idea.

"She was blacked out," said Justin, when I quietly recounted the story to him later that day at the Happy Bubble.

"What's that?" I asked.

"That's when you're so drunk you're walking around, but you don't know what you're doing. Your brain's shut down, but the rest of you is still going."

I'd never heard of this, but then I remembered times when my mother would show up late at night and be in a similar kind of trance. You'd talk to her, and she didn't seem to hear you. I always assumed she didn't want to be bothered right then. But maybe she was "blacked out."

"And Phoebe?" said Justin. "That's nothin' new. I've seen her like that. She's a party girl. She's hard-core."

We were cleaning the windows of a Jeep Cherokee as we talked.

"Yeah but she was lying on the beach," I said. "Like right on the sand, under an old sleeping bag. Something could have happened to her."

Justin laughed, then checked himself. "Hey. I feel you. You gotta be careful. Sometimes weird shit happens. You wake up somewhere, and you don't know where you are or how you got there. It's happened to me. Woke up by some train tracks in Vernonia once. Had to hitchhike home."

The fact that Justin had done the same thing didn't exactly make me feel better.

"She looked like she was dead," I said, my voice tightening with emotion.

Justin shrugged. "She's all right," he said. "She'll learn. Or she won't. Ain't nothin' you can do about it. That's how it goes with some chicks. They don't know when to stop."

I nodded at this. I'd already decided not to tell anyone else about finding Phoebe on the beach. I didn't want to seem like a gossip or someone who talked about people in their most embarrassing moments. But I still had the image in my brain. The sight of her on the sand, the strange stillness of her body, the deathly pallor of her skin. And worst of all, her eyes after she'd woken up: the way they'd looked right through me, as if I wasn't there.

PART TWO

JULY

The weird thing about finding Phoebe on the beach was
how quickly I forgot about it. I mean, I *didn't* forget about
it, not at all; it was just so strange, so surreal, it very quickly
became like a dream in my head. When I considered that
Phoebe never once spoke to me that morning and, according
to Justin, would probably not remember what happened, this
made it even more dreamlike. It was as if the whole thing
happened in my sleep. I knew it hadn't. But it felt like it had.

Instead of Phoebe, I spent the next day thinking about
Jace. And her kiss. *That* felt real. People knew it happened
and would remember it. Which meant I needed to deal
with it.

The main question was, could Jace and I go out? I
honestly didn't know. When I pictured us together, what I
mostly saw was us being friends, talking, having a coffee,

her being a person I would sit with at beach parties.

But maybe I needed to give the romantic side a chance. Maybe I needed to kiss her again. But how could I do that? I'd already blown it with her in the car. Now she probably assumed I *didn't* want to kiss her. Could I just say something? Tell her that I wasn't sure, that I didn't know how I felt exactly?

One day went by, and then another. I could sense Emily watching me around the house. Since she and Jace were friends, they had no doubt discussed the situation. So far Emily hadn't said a word. It made for some interesting meals: Uncle Rob and Aunt Judy sitting there oblivious, Emily pretending she didn't know about the kiss, me pretending I didn't know she knew about the kiss. I wondered if she might break down and say to me, *So what's up? Do you like Jace or not?* but Emily was too cool for that.

Then Kelsey saved me by turning sixteen. Her birthday was July 2, and she was having a bowling party to celebrate. Jace and Emily and I were all invited. This would be our chance to hang out again in a casual way. Hopefully, this would make it clearer what I should do.

I drove Emily to the party in her mom's Toyota. On the way over Emily put on extra lip gloss. I was wearing a new Western shirt I'd bought at Bill's Army-Navy, since that's what all the other guys in Seaside wore. I was excited to see Jace. I really did like her. But I still didn't know what would happen.

We parked and went inside Sunset Lanes. We were instantly surrounded by the sounds of crashing pins and gliding balls. Classic rock played loudly from the ceiling. The bowling alley had that same time-warp feel as Freezie Burger. It looked like an eighties movie, with neon lights and old beer signs and pinball machines. You never knew if they were doing this on purpose, or if Seaside people just never got around to replacing anything.

Emily and I got our bowling shoes. When we approached the others, I saw Jace, but I got nervous and didn't talk to her. Then we had to pick out bowling balls. Emily and I wanted the same ball, but when I said we could share it, she said no, she wasn't sharing. So then I had to walk around to the other lanes to find my own ball, which took a while. I finally picked one, which still didn't fit my fingers as well as the one Emily had. So now I was mad at Emily.

We split into teams with four people each. Jace was on the other team. Once we were actually bowling I tried to look at her, but now she was acting shy and wouldn't look at me. So then it was weird for the first game, not *terrible* weird, just two people having a case of nerves.

After the first game we switched the teams, and Jace was on my team. I tried sitting next to her, but when I did, she looked away and then got up and stood in the back with Lauren. Had I offended her somehow? Did she think I didn't like her now, just because I had hesitated when she kissed me? There was no way to tell.

So I waited until the next game and then tried to

casually ask her about the library, like what her hours were. I was going to say, *I'll come by sometime.* But just as I was asking, she suddenly turned and walked away, and she seemed pissed off. So now I was totally confused. I thought, *Oh my God, I completely messed this up.* And then I was super embarrassed and avoided looking at Jace or Emily or anyone else. Also I was totally sucking at bowling. I got like an eighty-four on my last game, which was the worst I'd ever bowled.

When the party was over, everyone walked back toward the main entrance. People started saying good-bye. Jace was still there, and again I walked over to her, but when I got there, I felt so stupid I couldn't say anything. Kelsey came over and hugged Jace good-bye, and then Jace went to her car and drove away.

Emily said nothing through all of this. In the car I was so embarrassed, I didn't know what to do. Like could I say, *I like Jace—I just screwed up.* But now I didn't know if I did like her. Especially since she acted so pissed off. So I got nervous. Big deal. It happens. It was no reason for her to get mad.

Emily remained silent for the drive home. I felt like this was her way of telling me how bad I'd screwed up. When we got home, I went straight downstairs to the basement and threw myself on the bed. Talk about epic fail.

And then it was the Fourth of July. This was a big deal in Seaside, the highlight of the summer for the locals. Uncle Rob's family, who lived farther down the coast, came up every year to watch the big parade. They showed up that afternoon, two parents, one aunt, one grandmother, and five little kids. The Happy Bubble was closed, so I was home too. Emily had disappeared earlier, and Kyle was at Oregon State with the baseball team, but still, with five little kids running around, the house turned to total chaos. I bailed and walked into town and tried to read my book at the coffee shop. But even there the excitement of the Fourth was taking over. I kept checking my phone, too, hoping Emily might text and tell me what she and Jace were doing later, but so far I had heard nothing.

So then at seven thirty I walked up Broadway to where my uncle Rob's family had saved a spot for the parade. They had chairs set up and blankets and a cooler with drinks and snacks. So then, since I hadn't heard from Jace or Emily, I settled in with them. With just a few minutes before it began, I texted Emily:

Are you guys coming to the parade?

She wrote back a few seconds later.

No.

That's all it said. *No.* Obviously they were pissed. How embarrassing. Jesus. Well, what could I do? I hadn't done anything wrong. I stuffed my phone into my pocket and stared grimly into the street.

The parade started. Some little kids walked by with a banner that said the first Seaside Fourth of July parade was held in 1904. I was like, *Thanks for the history lesson.* After that some cowgirls marched by with flags. Then the Seaside High School marching band went by playing "Crazy Train," which they could barely get through. Then a fire truck went by and some cops on horses.

I got out my phone and checked my messages. Still nothing from Jace or Emily.

A guy wearing a Santa suit rode by on the back of a convertible; I looked around at the other bystanders. Santa

Claus on the Fourth of July? Was I the only one who thought that was weird?

After that some seven-year-olds dressed like ladybugs appeared. The poor kids didn't seem to understand the concept of "parade" and were wandering all over the place, stopping to talk to people, eating ice cream cones. One of them was dragging his wings behind him. Another wanted to go home and started crying when his mother explained he had to keep walking.

I checked my phone again. Still no messages. Now I was getting pissed. This wasn't fair. Jace and I were friends. And now what? We were never going to speak again? Just because I was caught off guard by a kiss?

Last was a middle school girls' baton team. They were having problems too. One girl threw her baton up in the air, and it came down and hit the girl behind her on the head. . . .

After the parade the Reilly clan packed up their stuff. I was in a terrible mood. I told Aunt Judy I was going down to the beach, since that's where the fireworks supposedly were.

My mood got worse at the beach. The Promenade was packed with tourists. There were gangs of high school dudes cruising around and girls shrieking and younger kids chasing each other through the crowds. Everyone was having a great time, which made me even more pissed than I already was. When three prep guys wouldn't give me room to pass, I knocked shoulders with one of them. The guy immediately stopped and gave me a look like, *What?* He meant it too—he wanted to fight. But I kept walking, and his friends pulled him back. "Forget it man, he's just some asshole local. . . ."

Farther down the Promenade, I heard someone call my name. I looked up and saw Justin and Tyler. There was a whole gang of them, Justin and his buddies, sitting on the Promenade railing, watching the people walk by. They were drinking beers and not bothering to hide them since the Promenade was so jammed with people. "Nick! Hey!" said Justin. He waved me over.

I have to admit, I was very happy to see his face. I went over to the group of them. Someone handed me a beer.

"You havin' a good Fourth?" said Justin.

I made a vague shrug. "I got stuck watching the parade," I said.

"The parade?" laughed Justin. "Now why would you do that?"

"The babes are right here!" said Tyler.

He was right about that. We all stopped talking to watch a pack of beautiful blond high school girls stream past us.

"Would you look at that . . . ," said one of Justin's other friends.

"Hey, ladies!" called out another.

"To the girls!" said Justin, raising his beer and then guzzling it.

We all drank in unison. It felt good, the beer going down, the fizz and the burn. My chest, which felt like it was about to explode a moment before, went calm.

I had just settled back against the stone railing when a hand reached out of the crowd and slapped the beer out of my hand. It hit me in the foot and sprayed all over my leg.

It was the guy from before, the prep guy who I'd knocked into. He was suddenly right in my face. "You should watch where you're going!" he snarled. He was my age, gelled hair, polo shirt. He grabbed the front of my shirt and pushed me hard into the railing.

"Hey!" said Justin, jumping in. He grabbed the guy's arm, and the three of us became tangled in a three-way shoving match. At the same time Justin's other friends hopped down off the rail and snuck around behind the guy. They got him around the neck, yanked him backward and slammed him to the ground.

Then they beat him. Like seriously. Four against one. Punching, kicking, kicking in the face. I couldn't believe how vicious they were. I thought they might kill him.

The prep guy's friends came running up but stopped immediately when they saw what was happening. They began backing away, screaming for the police.

The whole thing lasted about three seconds, and then Justin and his friends took off running down the Promenade. I was still frozen in place, staring at the prep guy. He was rolling on the ground. His face was a bloody mess.

By then the flow of tourists had stopped, and people had their phones out to film the guy. I could hear Justin's crew running away, whooping and hollering like wild animals. I realized I better do the same. I took off after them.

I ran fast. I was supercharged with adrenaline: the shock of the beating, the thrill of the escape.

I finally caught up with Justin and Tyler, and the three of us ducked behind a wood fence and struggled to catch our breath. I had never run so fast in my life. I had to lean against a tree to steady myself.

Justin smiled at me. "You okay, Nick?"

I was shaking slightly, trembling in my legs. "Yeah, I think so," I gasped. "Sorry to get you involved in that. That was my fight."

"Sorry?" said Justin. "Are you kidding? That was awesome! I love kickin' me some tourist ass!"

Tyler seemed to agree with this. He was grinning ear to ear.

Justin reached into his coat pocket and pulled out a can of beer. He popped the top, and it sprayed beer all over.

"That was *crazy*," I finally managed to say.

"He asked for it . . . ," said Tyler with a shrug.

"That guy won't be pickin' on any locals any time soon," said Justin. He took a long swig of the beer and belched loudly. He handed me the beer and I drank too.

"Whaddaya doing now?" Justin asked me. "You gotta go home or you wanna go to a party?"

I looked at him. I looked back up the Promenade. "I wanna go to a party."

20

Justin, Tyler, and I snuck back into the center of town, weaving our way through the tourist hordes. We made it to Tyler's pickup and climbed into the cab. Justin grabbed a fresh pint of whiskey from the glove box and cracked it open.

Tyler had parked in the Ace Hardware parking lot, and we found ourselves stuck behind some other cars, which were also stuck, because of the crowds in the street. After a few minutes of waiting, Tyler turned the truck around and drove up and over the sidewalk behind us, squeezing between two parking meters and then dropping down into the street with such force, we all bounced up and hit our heads on the cab's ceiling.

Tyler floored it, and we roared out of there, speeding along for two blocks before we got stuck in another traffic jam, since there were so many cars trying to get on the highway. "Now we're screwed," said Justin. There seemed no other remedy for the traffic jam than more whiskey and a joint, which Justin fired up. I took a hit. Tyler took a hit. Justin took a hit. Around it went, while outside on the street, people ran between cars, swung around parking meters, yelled and whooped and caused whatever chaos they could. Two younger kids jumped onto our back bumper, rocked us up and down a few times, and then jumped off.

"Fourth of July," said Justin with a big stoned smile. "You gotta love it."

We finally got out of Seaside, and Tyler gunned it down the highway. We drove twenty minutes, uphill into the mountains, and then took a left onto a gravel road, which turned into a dirt road, which turned into a *narrow* dirt road. Another truck appeared, speeding the other way, and for a moment I didn't see how both trucks could squeeze by each other. But Tyler floored it and swerved off the road on the right, and the other truck skidded into the dirt on the left, and somehow the side mirrors didn't hit. The other truck was full of laughing, screaming partiers, with Metallica blasting out the windows.

We arrived at a wide clearing at the base of a mountain. There was a farmhouse and some other buildings and a large barn. Tyler parked in a field full of other cars, and we tumbled out of the cab. The air up there smelled delicious: cold and clean and full of adventure. I thought so anyway, stoned and drunk as I was.

A large bonfire crackled just behind the farmhouse, and beyond that you could see the open doors of the barn and a crowd of people milling around. As we got closer, loud electric guitar chords blasted out through the barn doors. A drumbeat began to play. "Sounds like we're just in time!" said Tyler.

Before we went in, though, we hit the food tables by the bonfire. On two long plastic tables were chips, chili, Cheez Doodles, a plate of cold-looking hamburgers, and several hot dogs that were rolling around loose. I was suddenly famished, so I folded a hamburger bun around a hot dog and added some egg salad and salsa and ate that. Justin and Tyler also picked through whatever they could find, stuffing their faces and chewing with their mouths open.

So then it was into the barn. The band was a bunch of scraggly, gray-haired guys standing on a stage made of hay bales and plywood. They didn't look very professional, but they sounded pretty good. They started playing "Sweet Emotion," and the mostly older crowd went wild. It was a pretty rough-looking bunch: forty-year-old women with cowboy hats and short-shorts and lots of cleavage, most of them sloppy drunk, *yahoo*ing and holding up their Bud Lights, while their balding boyfriends stood around with their beer guts and black leather biker vests. Tyler started jumping around, doing a weird hippy dance. Justin laughed at him. I just stood there, taking it all in. *These are the mountain people,* I thought, as a guy beside me stirred his drink with a hunting knife.

At one point I went outside to piss. Even that was its own special thrill: standing under the stars, staring straight up the face of a mountain, amazed at how far away from home I was, how young I was, how strong and full of life I felt. *Holy shit,* I thought, *I'm seventeen years old!*

Stumbling back toward the barn, I noticed there was a whole other party happening in the farmhouse. I decided to check that out. I circled around the bonfire and went in. It was loud inside. People were drinking and yakking and smoking cigarettes. One of the counter girls from the Freezie Burger was there, and the skinny guy who made the sandwiches at the coffee shop.

I made my way to the kitchen, where I snagged a fresh beer from an ice-filled plastic tub. I didn't know anyone, not well enough to talk to, so I cracked open my beer and took a deep swig. That was when I heard a familiar female shriek. Nicole! I moved out of the way, as she came crashing into the kitchen. And then, behind her, was Phoebe. The sight of her hit me like an electric jolt. Nicole was doing her brassy party girl thing, but Phoebe looked like a rock star. Short skirt, lipstick, eyeliner. And that cocky smirk on her face. Like, *Whatever, losers, get out of my way.*

I watched the two of them pass through the kitchen

into the large playroom area behind it, which was empty except for a handful of people standing around.

"What's going on!?" said Nicole loudly. "I thought there's supposed to be dancing!"

"There is! There is!" said someone.

"Well put on some music!"

Two guys hurried over to a bookcase to figure out the music.

Phoebe and Nicole stood waiting. Some other people also entered the room, apparently wanting to dance too. Phoebe took a sip from her beer. Nicole started yelling at someone.

I wondered if I could go in there and start a conversation with them. Phoebe was the one I really wanted to talk to. I didn't see how I could, though, so I stayed where I was, in the kitchen, next to a bowl of pretzels, nervously grabbing handfuls and munching them down.

Meanwhile an older guy came over and started eating pretzels too. He said he recognized me from the Happy Bubble and began telling me a story about Uncle Rob. I was like, *Yeah, right, whatever.* As he talked, Phoebe came back into the kitchen. I made room for her at the pretzel bowl, smiling at her, since I was still pretty drunk and feeling brave. She smiled back and reached into the bowl. She stood there with me and the older guy, chomping pretzels.

"You're Phoebe," I said.

"That's right," she said, without looking at me.

The old guy was still talking, but I ignored him. Phoebe ignored him too.

"I'm Nick," I said.

"Hi, Nick," she said.

There was this amazing moment of silence. Except for the old guy, who was still talking. And the general noise of the party. But I didn't hear any of that.

"Do you remember me?" I asked her.

She glanced at me once. "No," she said. "Should I?"

"I met you at the beach party?"

"Oh yeah?"

My heart began to thump in my chest. "It was actually *after* the beach party," I said. "You probably don't remember."

"I guess not."

"I'm Kyle's cousin."

That got her attention. "Really?" she said, studying me more closely. "I didn't know Kyle had a cousin."

"Yeah. We're cousins."

"You sorta look like him."

"Do I?" I said, blushing.

"I dunno, maybe not," she said, nibbling a pretzel in a flirty way.

Now I could barely breathe I was so excited. I took a deep swig off my beer.

In the other room they'd figured out the music. Someone turned down the lights in the playroom. "Bust a Move" began to play. Phoebe and I watched while Nicole and some other people began to bob their heads to the beat.

Here's a tale for all the fellas
Tryin' to do what ladies tell us

"Do you like to dance?" Phoebe asked me.

I nodded that I did.

Phoebe began to turn back and forth to the music. She took another drag off her own beer. Then she reached out and grabbed my arm. "C'mon," she said.

She pulled me into the playroom, then released me and began to dance with Nicole. I fell in with the two of them. More people joined in; they came pouring in from the rest of the house. It was true what they said: Wherever Phoebe and Nicole were, that's where the party was.

I stayed near the two of them. Phoebe moved around in a bored way, not taking any of it too seriously. She drank her beer as she danced. Then she grabbed my elbow and pulled me close. "What's your name again?" she yelled over the music. I could feel the warmth of her breath on my face.

"Nick," I said into her ear.

"Nick," she repeated.

Then she turned away and danced and ignored everyone else. Which is what I did too. That was the best strategy, I figured: act as if nothing was happening, that this wasn't a big deal. Though in fact everything was happening. My whole life was happening. It was a very big deal.

It was easy to lose yourself around Phoebe and Nicole.
They were so cool, so funny, so at ease with everything. This
was their life. Cigarettes. Drinks. Music. The eyes of every
guy and most of the girls on them. It wasn't a life with a lot of
future—I understood that. But what was the future anyway?
Did it even exist?

The three of us danced for one song and then another
and then another. When a slow song came on, I stood with
them and drank my beer and kept my mouth shut. When
we eventually took a break, they pulled me with them to a
couch, and sat on either side of me.

"So you're Kyle's cousin!" Nicole said to me, in her
loud, saucy voice.

I nodded.

"I can see the resemblance," she said. She pushed her

shoulder into mine. "Do you know who I am?"

"I think so."

"I'm Kyle's great high school love!"

"I've heard that," I said.

"You have?" she said with concern. "From who?"

I shrugged. "Everyone," I said. "You're famous."

She laughed. "Oh my God! I sort of am, aren't I? Ha-ha.
I like you. I don't even know you, but I like you already!"

"I like you too," I said.

"And you know why we broke up, don't you?" she said.

"No . . ."

"His *coach* didn't like me. It was his coach! And Kyle's
such a big-shot baseball player and all. . . ." She did a pout-
face to emphasize the unfairness of this. "And Kyle always
does what his coaches tell him. Because he's like that. He's
a Boy Scout basically. People think he's *so big and strong*,
but he's a Boy Scout. He's afraid of me, is the real problem.
He didn't know what to do with me. Because I do what
I want and I speak my mind. And I don't take shit from
nobody! That's something you need to know about me."

"Okay," I said.

She sighed. "But anyways, so yeah, we were in love.
We still are. He tries to pretend we're not, but I know. Girls
know that sort of thing."

I nodded.

"What about you?" she asked me, tapping my thigh
with her pointy fingernail. "Do you have a girlfriend?"

"I did."

"What happened to her?"

I considered telling her, but then realized that would be a mistake. "We broke up," I said.

"What about now?" she said, leaning closer and turning slightly so that her large breasts mushed into me. "Are you *available*? Or has Phoebe already claimed you?"

"Uh . . ."

She leaned forward so she could see her friend. "*Phoebe!?*" she said loudly.

"Yeah?" said Phoebe, who was looking at her phone.

"Have you claimed Nick here?"

"What?" said Phoebe.

"I said, have you claimed Nick? Or is he still *available*?"

Phoebe shrugged.

"You know, he's Kyle's cousin," said Nicole.

"I know," said Phoebe. "I'm the one who told you that."

"Well do you like him or not?"

"He's okay."

"Just okay?"

Phoebe didn't answer. She didn't look up.

Nicole sat back on the couch. "Well I think you're *adorable*," she whispered into the side of my face. Her breath smelled like beer and cigarettes. "Unfortunately, with you being Kyle's stepbrother and all . . ."

"*Cousin*," I said. "I'm his cousin."

"Well, either way, it might be a little *incestuous*. . . ."

I didn't say anything more. A new song came on, but nobody got up to dance. Nicole spotted someone she knew in the kitchen. She began waving wildly, and jumped up and launched herself in that direction. Phoebe, left alone with me, said nothing and continued to study her phone.

A few minutes later, though, Phoebe put her phone away. She actually smiled at me for a moment as she did. Then she scooted a little closer and casually put her arm along the top of the couch behind me. I could feel her fingers graze the side of my face when she did it. We sat like that for a few moments, watching the dancers, her hand behind my head. Then she began to *touch* my hair and the back of my neck.

Suddenly, I wasn't so drunk anymore. I wasn't sure what she was doing. Her fingers burrowed down to my scalp and began to massage the base of my skull. It felt amazing. I glanced over at her once; she grinned. I grinned. She began to do it more, stroking my hair, caressing my neck. It sent warm shivers all through me.

She wants me to kiss her, I thought. I had to do it. I couldn't wait. I couldn't hesitate. I turned toward her. She was already looking at my lips. I leaned in. Our mouths connected. Our lips touched, and then our tongues. And just like that it was happening. I was making out with Phoebe, right in the middle of this huge party.

It was heavenly. But I was too excited. I was going too fast. Phoebe was going slower; she was more of a delicate kisser. I followed her lead. I slowed down. And then it got even better. Her lips were so soft, and yet firm, and they fit so well with mine. And the feeling of it, the idea of it: this beautiful girl, this *wild* girl, with her pretty face and luminous skin. Phoebe, the girl I thought I'd never even talk to, she was right here in my arms!

After a minute or two Phoebe pulled away. It took me a second to open my eyes, and when I did, I saw that she was sitting back. So I sat back too. She wasn't looking at me now; she was staring at the dancers. I did the same. My whole body was humming, electrified, but I did my best to continue my original strategy. *Nothing happening here. No need to talk. No need to do anything.*

Some new people were dancing. Others were standing around. Phoebe lit a cigarette and checked her phone. I remained focused on the dancers and the other people. I noticed an older guy across the room, staring hard at Phoebe and me. He looked pissed off, or maybe jealous. I wondered who he was.

Nicole came back to the couch and said something urgent to Phoebe, who instantly stood up. Before I could react, the two of them had crossed the room and disappeared into the kitchen. The guy staring at us had left too, I noticed. I wasn't sure what was happening, so I stayed where I was. Probably they would come back. And anyway, it wouldn't have felt right to jump up and chase after them. My super-chill approach had worked so far. I felt like I better stick with it.

But after ten minutes passed, with no sign of them, I wasn't so sure. After fifteen minutes I casually got to my feet, went into the kitchen. I looked around. They were not in the kitchen.

I moved toward the front of the house. There were clusters of partiers in different rooms. I calmly checked each area, but there was no sign of them. I began to move a little faster, and when I'd covered the whole house, I returned once more to the playroom. No Nicole. No Phoebe.

I went outside. The bonfire had died down. The food table was still there, but even more trashed then before. I scanned the grounds, the fields, the cars parked along the edge of the woods. No Phoebe. No Nicole.

Okay, I said to myself, *so she left.* Was that so bad? The important thing was: Phoebe and I had made out. And I hadn't done anything stupid. Which meant that she knew me now, she would remember me, we could possibly make out again . . . if she didn't have a boyfriend. I hadn't asked anyone if she did. That would be good information to have.

I walked back into the barn. The band was taking a break, but there were still people standing around or sitting on hay bales. I spotted Tyler and Justin, sitting on the ground along the back wall. "Hey," I said, kneeling on the hard dirt.

They raised their plastic beer cups in greeting. "Where you been?" said Justin.

"In the house," I said. "You'll never believe what just happened to me."

"What?"

"I made out with Phoebe!"

They both stared at me. They didn't seem as excited as I thought they'd be.

"Phoebe? Phoebe Garnet?" said Justin, sitting up slightly. Tyler sat up too.

"I guess so," I said. "You know, *Phoebe*, Nicole's friend."

"Yeah," said Justin. "That's her."

"Phoebe Garnet," said Tyler, without enthusiasm. "Yeah. She's hot."

"Are you kidding?" I said. "She's *totally hot*."

"Where was this?" asked Justin.

"In the house," I said. I was getting excited as it began to sink in. *I'd hooked up with the hottest girl at the whole party.*

"The only thing is," I said. "Does she have a boyfriend?"

Tyler looked at Justin. Justin looked at Tyler.

"Do you guys know if she does or not?"

"I don't know," said Justin.

Tyler shrugged.

"Some older guy was staring at us," I said. "He looked jealous."

Neither Tyler nor Justin said anything. I didn't understand what their problem was. How did they not see the importance of this?

But whatever. I didn't care. I stopped talking and took a seat next to Tyler, leaning against the wall and looking out. I stared into the rafters of the barn and thought about the taste of Phoebe's lips, her distinctive kissing style. And the way she'd caressed the back of my neck: That was definitely a serious move, an *adult* move. It had felt incredible. I should have done it back to her. I would next time. If there was a next time.

"You got any more of that whiskey?" I asked Justin.

"Nah, dude, we're tapped out," he said, showing me the empty bottle.

That was too bad. I could have used one last shot to calm me down.

A country-western song began to play over the PA speakers. I didn't know the song, but I nodded my head to the rhythm. The lyric was about falling in love. The sweet pain of it. The helplessness. I immediately went into a kind of trance, sitting there on the hard dirt, in the barn, my heart filled to bursting with the idea of Phoebe Garnet.

I was in a strange mood at the car wash on Monday. I did my work. I vacuumed the cars and swept the office. During breaks I sat with my coworkers but didn't speak. I guess I was excited about Phoebe. But I was also a little in shock. What had happened exactly? And what did it mean?

At noon I walked down to Freezie Burger and got everybody lunch. Later, when I finished my shift, I slipped out and walked to the coffee shop and got a caffe mocha. I sat by the window and watched the people walking by. These were tourists mostly, forty-year-old parents, their ten-year-old kids, the ages when nothing really happens in life. Not like the age I was now, when everything happens, everything important at least.

The skinny guy who made the sandwiches saw me as he was wiping down the tables. He'd seen me at the party. He gave me a little head nod, and I nodded back. But I didn't want to talk to anyone. I wanted to think about Phoebe.

This went on for the next couple days: my body numbly going through my daily routine while my brain immersed itself in the concept of Phoebe. Oddly enough, I had no desire to actually see her. That would break the spell. For now, I just wanted to *think* about her.

I made up conversations in my head, long talks we would have at some time in the future. I thought about dates we could go on (did a girl like that even go on dates?). Best of all, I replayed every detail of our time on the couch: her fingers in my hair, the look on her face as she came in for the kiss, the smell of her, the warm softness of her slender body.

Occasionally I'd have to interact with other people. This was an annoyance. To talk to Aunt Judy or Justin or the customers at the car wash required that I shut down my Phoebe dreams and refocus and listen to what they were saying. This I found highly irritating. And what they wanted was never important anyway. Nothing was important except Phoebe.

And then one night, as we were closing, Emily and Jace pulled into the Happy Bubble. The sight of Jace's car snapped me back to reality.

Emily came into the office. "Jace and I are going to the Sandpiper," she said. "Do you want to come?"

"Yeah," I said quickly. "Sure."

I hadn't seen Jace since Kelsey's birthday party. I hoped this meant we were all going to be friends again. Despite the Phoebe stuff, I missed hanging out with the two of them. They had become my two best friends, in a way.

I finished my closing duties and went out. I got in the back seat of Jace's car. "Hey," I said to Jace, making sure to catch her eye in the rearview mirror.

"Hey," she said, looking back at me. Our eyes met and held for a moment. It appeared we were back on good terms. Which was a relief.

At the Sandpiper, we talked about their Fourth of July adventures. They'd gone to a party in Astoria but a thick wall of fog had rolled in and ruined the fireworks.

I mentioned that I'd hung out with Justin and his friends, but I didn't say anything else. I didn't mention Phoebe. I didn't know what they would think. Besides, I didn't want to make Jace jealous. Not that Jace and I were going to be together. We were obviously in "friends" territory now. But still.

When we were leaving the Sandpiper, Emily went to the bathroom, and Jace and I waited by the cash registers. As we stood there, Jace turned to me. "There's something I wanted to ask you," she said. "It's sort of a weird request."

"Okay," I said.

"Would you want to have dinner with me in Gearhart? At the Pacific Grill?"

That *was* a weird request. "Dinner?" I said. "Is it a special occasion?"

"No. I've just always wanted to go there, and I never have."

"Oh," I said.

"I've got some money from working at the library . . . and that's what I want to blow it on."

"And it's in Gearhart?"

"Yeah. The Pacific Grill."

She could see I was still confused.

"It wouldn't be like a date or anything," she explained. "I just want to go. I asked my parents to take me for my birthday. But they didn't want to."

"Why not?" I said.

"They thought it would be too snobby."

"Oh."

"It *is* kind of snobby."

"Yeah, if it's in Gearhart," I said.

"That's why I figured you might want to go. You've probably been to places like that."

I wasn't sure I had been. But then I thought about it. I'd been to Harrison's a few times, which was Eugene's most expensive restaurant. And I'd been to the Arbor, the other fancy place that people liked. These were usually celebration dinners, involving some career success of my mother's.

I looked at Jace, who was staring at the pies in the counter display. "Yeah, okay," I said.

"I mean, you don't have to," said Jace. "But if you feel like it."

"No," I said. "That sounds fun."

* * *

After the Sandpiper, we went to Newport, another beach town a couple hours to the south. They made a special salt-water taffy there, which was Emily's favorite.

Jace drove. The two of them talked. I sat in the back seat and thought about Phoebe. It was so fun to do that. To just go somewhere quiet, somewhere with something interesting to look at, and drown myself in thoughts of Phoebe. Was it possible that I was already in love with her? After one night, one kiss? And who exactly had I fallen in love with? And what would it be like, the two of us together? Like on a day-to-day level? It felt so satisfying to ponder these questions. To stare out the window at the passing trees and the endless ocean, and think about her face, her lips, her eyes.

In Newport, we went to the candy store and got the special taffy. It didn't taste any different from the taffy in Seaside, I noticed. But Emily was like that; she had to have her special things. We sat on the bench outside the candy store and chewed the taffy and watched the tourists. Newport was more elegant than Seaside, more historical. I wondered if Phoebe had ever been here. Maybe she and I could go there together.

Driving home, Jace and Emily were talking about different couples they knew and what happened when people had sex or lost their virginity. I joined into this discussion, arguing with Emily mostly, about what a boy "owed" a girl if they had sex. Jace and I were both saying that nobody "owed" anyone anything, you just had to figure it out within the relationship.

This got me thinking about Kate again. I was still pissed she wasn't my first. Instead, it'd been Lindsey Clarke. She was this wild-child prep girl—her father was a big-deal physics professor in Eugene. We were smoking weed one night at a friend's house, when I made a joke about still being a virgin. Lindsey got very excited and took my hand and led me upstairs to the parents' bedroom. And that was the end of my virginity.

Lindsey and I tried going out after that. We went snow-boarding a couple times. But we didn't have enough in common. And she didn't want a steady boyfriend anyway. She was super nice about it, and we stayed friends. But it still felt disappointing.

The other girl I'd had sex with was Haley Ross. This happened over spring break at a hotel in Mexico. My dad had taken us there, since Mom was at her fancy rehab in California. Dad figured if she was getting the spa treatment, then we should too. Haley was from Illinois, and her family was rich, it sounded like. We met at the pool and ended up making out on the roof that night. She had a strange personality. She didn't like to talk. If you asked her questions about herself, she got very nervous. The morning after the roof, when I saw her at breakfast, she wouldn't even look at me. Later, though, she called me on the hotel phone and wanted to meet back up there. This time we had sex, on one of those chaise-longue chairs, in the bright Mexican moonlight. I think she cried afterward, though she denied it. I could tell something was up with her; you could see it in her face, some sort of psychological issue. Dr. Snow and I talked about it.

So yeah, that was it, my entire sexual history. A couple times with Lindsey who was more just a friend. And once with Haley. It was fine, I guess. And there was nothing I could do about it anyway. People have sex for a million different reasons, sometimes with people they barely know or care about. So I wasn't that different from anybody else.

The next day was cloudy and cold. Not much was going on at the Happy Bubble until Carson and Wyatt pulled in, in the Camaro.

They'd never come in when I was there. They wanted a car wash. They were old friends of Justin's, and since Kyle wasn't there, or Uncle Rob, Justin ran them through for free. When they came out of the other side, Justin let them use the vacuum as well.

Carson and Wyatt seemed more normal to me this time. Not like people I would actually be friends with, but more like ordinary stoner dudes. We had plenty of those at my high school. They were usually nice enough guys. They'd flunk their biology tests and then laugh about it over bong hits in the parking lot.

"Yeah, you missed the big Fourth of July party at the

Andersons'," said Justin. There were still no customers, so we were standing around the Camaro while Wyatt tried to fix the broken armrest on the driver's door.

"I heard you kicked some guy's ass on the Promenade," said Wyatt, kneeling and inspecting the open door.

"Oh, yeah," said Justin with casual humility. "We got into it a little."

"Who started it?" asked Wyatt.

"Some dude. He came at Nick here," he said, nodding toward me.

I blushed slightly.

"We took care of it," said Justin, shrugging. "We kinda had 'em outnumbered."

"What happened at the Anderson place?" asked Carson, changing the subject.

"Nothin' really," said Justin. "They had the band going . . . the usual crowd."

"They were rockin' to the oldies," I said, since I hadn't said anything.

"Dylan's mom got up there," said Justin. "Sang a couple songs."

"Buncha old farts," said Carson.

"*Sweet home Al-abama,*" sang Justin.

Everyone chuckled.

"It was all right," said Justin. "There were some younger chicks too."

I waited for someone to say something about Phoebe and Nicole. Maybe Justin would tell Carson and Wyatt what had happened to me. But suddenly Wyatt, who had been gently tugging on the armrest, broke it off completely.

"For fuck's sake!" said Wyatt, holding the armrest in his hand. "I knew that would happen."

"*Dude,*" said Carson.

"Did you mean to do that?" asked Justin.

"*No,*" said Wyatt.

We all stood watching as Wyatt studied the screw hole that had rotted out. A dry yellowy substance was leaking from it. He touched it with his finger.

The door panel was in pretty bad shape, as was the rest of the Camaro. The rips in the seats were duct-taped. The worn out floor carpet was covered with mismatched pieces of household carpet. The entire car was a patchwork.

Wyatt shifted into a full sitting position and stared at the door, considering his options.

"Did you hear Ryan is finally selling that old Mustang?" Carson told Justin.

"No way," said Justin. "That rusted out piece of shit?"

"I know," said Carson. "He claims it runs, but it's been sitting there since his brother bought it."

"That thing'll never run," said Wyatt.

"I guess he found some tech guy from Seattle," continued Carson. "The guy's gonna drive down and haul it back up there and restore it."

"Wow," said Justin. "I wonder how much?"

"Ryan said two grand."

"Two *grand*?" gasped Justin. "For that?"

"I wouldn't give you two hundred," said Wyatt. He was still poking at the door with his screwdriver.

"Ryan said the guy's from back east somewhere," said Carson. "Got that sound in his voice."

"What sound is that?" said Justin.

"You know. Lots of money. And no frickin' clue."

"Sounds about right," said Justin.

Carson continued: "So Ryan says to the guy, 'So you gonna do the restoring yourself,' and the guy says he's gonna pay this other guy to do it. And so Ryan's like, 'So you just wanna ride around in it?' And the guy says no, he only drives German cars, but his wife wants it because her first boyfriend had one."

"Yeah," said Wyatt, from the ground. "She probably got her first piece of ass in it."

"And you know *that* guy wasn't some computer geek," said Carson.

"Money don't change things," said Wyatt. "If you're a dork, you're a dork."

Everyone smiled at that.

"Kinda makes you wonder, though," said Carson, "what you'd do if you had that kinda money."

"I know what I'd do," said Justin.

"What's that?" asked Carson.

"I'd buy a restaurant."

"A restaurant? What do you know about restaurants?"

"Or a bar maybe," said Justin. "Someplace I could hang out. Drink for free."

"If you own the bar, then you're not drinking for free."

"You know what I mean," said Justin. "Why? What would you do?"

"I'd buy a boat," said Carson.

"Like a fishing boat?"

"No man, like a chick boat. Like to take chicks out in."

"I wouldn't do nothin' different," said Wyatt, holding the armrest in place. He was going to try to reattach it with the one screw that still worked.

"You get yourself a nice boat . . . ," said Carson. "Get some nice food . . . some fine wine . . . have some dudes in, like, servants' clothes."

"And where you gonna dock it?" asked Justin.

"California. Where else? That's where the girls are."

"Yeah," said Justin. "Chicks dig boats."

"Women like the finer things in life," said Carson. "And if you can provide those things . . ."

"You'd kinda have your pick then, wouldn't ya?" said Justin.

"You could have anything you want."

"Yeah, but what's the point?" I said. I hadn't meant to speak at that moment. The words just came out. "I mean, if all the girl wants is your boat and your money, why be with her?"

I saw Carson smile a little at that. Wyatt looked annoyed at his broken armrest.

"So you figure you're goin' more for the true love kinda thing . . . ?" Justin asked me.

I shrugged. "Why not? It's better than having someone use you."

"Yeah, but everybody uses people," said Justin. "That's how it works."

No one spoke for a moment.

"Nah, but I feel you," continued Justin. "A girl who loves you for who you are, like in your soul. I'd take that."

"Fuck yeah, I would too," said Carson.

"Still, the boat could be useful," reasoned Justin. "Like if there's an apocalypse or whatever."

"Shit," said Wyatt from behind his door. "You guys got any superglue in the office?"

For my dinner with Jace, I dug out my one nice button-down shirt, which I hadn't worn once in Seaside. I took a shower and put on extra Old Spice and combed my hair. Jace was wearing a yellow summer dress when she picked me up. Her long legs looked silky and smooth, and she smelled good too, like lemons. I felt nervous putting on my seat belt. Though officially this was not a date, it still felt like an "occasion" of some kind.

It took about ten minutes to get to Gearhart. It turned out Jace's mom was paying for our dinner as a birthday present, so Jace could keep her library money, so that was good.

The restaurant was on the main street. We pulled into the gravel parking lot in the back. I could see right away how fancy the Pacific Grill was. Even the gravel was perfectly clean, as if they'd polished every rock. A white picket fence surrounded the parking lot, with ivy growing over the top of it and little purple flowers.

A small sign and special lights directed you to a back door, which led to a passageway, which led around to the front of the restaurant. Jace had made us a reservation, so the hostess welcomed us with great formality. We followed her through the tables, which had white tablecloths and cloth napkins and multiple forks and spoons at each place. Jace and I were on our best behavior as we were seated at a table beside the window.

"Look at this silverware," Jace whispered after the hostess had left. "Is this the soup spoon?"

I didn't actually know which spoon was for what. "I think you just go from the outside toward the inside," I said. "Depending on what they bring."

Jace nodded and continued to study the different objects on our table. A man with a white coat and a bow tie appeared and gave us a basket of warm rolls wrapped in a crisp white napkin. Beside it, he presented us with a small bowl of iced butter chunks.

"Oh my God," said Jace, pulling the cloth back and breathing in the warm bread. "They just made these!"

She took a roll and I did too. We carefully tore them in half and took turns smearing butter on them. The light, fluffy dough practically melted in your mouth.

Our waitress looked like a fashion model, which made it hard to focus. I got tongue-tied. Jace ordered the seared tuna, and I ordered the free-range game hen. Then we sat there and giggled and watched the other dinner guests coming in. They were mostly older people, rich people, people who probably ate there all the time. A man with distinguished gray hair and a sport coat sat with his wife to our left. He looked like he'd never eaten anything except lavish meals at places like the Pacific Grill. It was fascinating to watch him. Jace watched him too. He snapped his napkin in the air before he put it in his lap. So then I tried snapping my napkin, and then Jace snapped hers. It was harder than it looked. Then we ate more of the delicious bread. When we'd used up all the butter, I proved my restaurant sophistication by waving to the water guy that we needed more. He brought it immediately.

After just the right amount of time, our dinners arrived. They were pretty spectacular. Jace and I compared notes and tasted each other's dishes. After a while we settled in and ate.

"So the Fourth of July, in Astoria . . . you got fogged out?" I asked. I had never got the full story.

"It was okay," said Jace, pulling her freshly washed hair back behind one ear. "They still shot off the fireworks. It was just so cold, and the grass was wet. We only went up there so Emily could see Oliver. He doesn't have his license, so we always have to visit him."

"What's he like?"

"He's nice. And he's cute. And he doesn't mind when Emily bosses him. But he also stands up to her sometimes, which is good too. I wanted to invite you to come with us, but Emily said no, since . . . you know . . ."

"Since what?"

"Since things got weird at Kelsey's birthday."

"Oh, right," I said. I had finished my meal and was dabbing my face with my napkin. "Sorry about that . . ."

"No, no, it was my fault," said Jace. "I was being weird. I could tell you wanted to talk to me."

"I totally did. I just wasn't sure—"

"It doesn't matter. I told Emily we were just friends anyway. But she was like, 'Nick didn't handle that right; he has to see that he made a mistake.' And I was saying that I made the same mistake you did. I was nervous! She always blames the guy though. . . ."

"Yeah, I noticed."

"She can afford to be like that. Since every boy likes her. But normal girls, people like me, we have to cut people slack. I mean, boys do stupid stuff all the time. That's practically their job in life. That's why they call them *boys*."

I laughed at this. Jace laughed too. We both sipped our sparkling waters. We were having a great time. No wonder the Pacific Grill cost so much. Everything that happened there somehow turned out perfect.

When our main course was gone, we ordered cappuccinos. As we sipped them, I found myself watching Jace. Not in a crushed-out way, just enjoying her intelligent face.

Afterward, we walked back through the parking lot, with the polished gravel and the tiny purple flowers. We were both feeling happy and full and satisfied. It made you wonder. Like, was the point of life to have the best of everything? The best meals, the best clothes, the best car? It kind of seemed like it was. It did at that moment anyway. But it also made me sad that Jace believed getting out of Seaside would make her life so much better. I mean, it would, in some ways, obviously. But I already had the life she wanted, and it hadn't worked out that great for me.

We drove back to Seaside, talking a little and then not. As we passed the WELCOME TO SEASIDE sign, I suddenly got an image of Phoebe in my head. I pictured her walking along the side of the road, by herself, as if she was a homeless person. I thought how if I was driving by, and I saw her like that, I would stop and offer her a ride. Not trying to get with her, but trying to be there for her, trying to show her that someone loved her and cared about her and that she was not alone.

25

I still hadn't tried to find or contact Phoebe. I guess I thought I'd see her somewhere—the car wash, another beach party, the Promenade. And the way she'd disappeared on me at the Fourth of July party, it made me think it would be the better move to not pursue her. Best to play it cool and wait until we ran into each other. This was Seaside; you pretty much saw everyone eventually.

The problem was: I *hadn't* seen her. And a lot of time had passed. I wasn't going to be here forever. So then one afternoon, after work, I decided to see if I could find her house. Maybe I could accidentally run into her that way.

I walked into the north-end neighborhood where she lived, which I remembered from driving her home from the beach. Unfortunately, I hadn't paid close attention that morning. I'd just followed her pointing finger. And I'd been so focused on her, I hadn't noticed any street signs or land-marks.

I walked down the first street I came to. I wasn't sure I would remember what her house looked like. According to my phone there were about ten blocks of these streets, three to four blocks deep, so it would take a while to cover all that ground.

I began my search. The houses were pretty old. They had that salty, weathered look. Faded paint, drooping roofs, sometimes a wind chime or a dream catcher in the front. It was fun to cover a neighborhood like that, taking your time, checking things out. A lady in her bathrobe was watering her weedy lawn. A guy in a dirty T-shirt lay on his side in his driveway, doing something to his motorcycle. Occasionally I'd see a house that looked like Phoebe's, and I would get nervous for a second. It seemed possible I might see her on the street. Or maybe she'd ride by on a bike, if she had a bike.

I walked up one crumbling street and down the next. There were potholes and broken asphalt and puddles. A wet breeze began to blow in off the ocean. Occasionally a scroungy dog would pass by. Or a damp cat.

I wondered what Kate would think of my recent adven-tures. Getting in fights. Hanging with the locals. Making out with dangerous, cigarette-smoking Phoebe. Kate would be supportive, as always, since she still loved me (I hoped she did; I still loved her). She'd say something like, *If you want to be a writer, I guess you need to experience things.*

But deep down she'd probably have her doubts. Seaside was such a different world from where she was, up on Orcas Island. She was probably playing tennis and going for swims and reading Jane Austen novels in a hammock. And probably a million interesting, good-looking guys were around, giving her rides on their scooters, sprawling on her freshly cut lawn at night. They'd be talking about colleges and their future lives. And around them the crickets would chirp, and the stars would shine, while the ocean, subdued up there among the islands, would calmly murmur and lap against the stones.

It hurt me to think about it. I tried not to. I reminded myself that Kate and I were following our separate paths. That's what Dr. Snow always said. He was big on "paths" and "journeys." We all have our different "roads" to travel, and sometimes it was impossible to predict where they would go, or why. The important thing was to stay open and learn whatever lessons came along. I smiled as I thought of the lessons I'd learned in Seaside: How to smoke out of a four-foot bong. How to beat a guy nearly to death. Where to find every last nickel in some California guy's Chevy Tahoe.

I didn't think about Kate too long. Maybe a minute or two before my mind, as usual, went back to Phoebe. Where was she on this windswept afternoon? Reckless, troubled Phoebe. Phoebe, whose eyes were green and whose lips tasted like smoke and alcohol and God knows what else. Her breath was so complicated, so ominous, and yet so alluring. It was like you were breathing in all her conflicts and contradictions. She was not a person you just "got" or would ever completely understand. Even Emily, who was also cute and a little bit *hard*, after you'd talked to her a couple times, you basically knew what her deal was. Or someone like Jace: Even in sarcasm mode it was obvious her heart was in the right place. But what about Phoebe? Where was her heart?

She and Nicole, they knew how to have a good time, that's for sure. The two of them, always at the center of things, always burning the brightest. Phoebe was what? Eighteen? She seemed older than that by about a thousand years. She was a very old soul. A person who knew things way sooner than she was supposed to. There were no girls like her at my high school. No girl would dare be like that. And finding her on the beach that morning, under the sleeping bag . . . sometimes I would remember that and I would be so amazed. That really happened! She had been dead asleep, *passed out*, on a beach at five thirty in the morning, on the cold sand, with the crabs and the seagulls, and the tide rolling up on her. It was bracing to remember that. This was not some ordinary person. Phoebe was like a character from a novel. She was a lost soul, a tragic figure, but also fearless and funny and strangely irresistible. And best of all: She had *let me into her world*. She had given me access. It felt exhilarating, that part of it. To be included in the excitement of her life. It proved I wasn't just some boring dude. I wasn't just some average Joe, with nothing going on.

*   *   *

I'd been walking about an hour when I saw a mailbox I thought I recognized. It had a special trim around the bottom. I studied the house and the driveway. When Phoebe got out of the truck that morning, she walked uphill, to the right, toward her front door. Which was consistent with this house, since the door was to the right of the driveway.

Was this it? The house was a dull reddish brown. Nobody appeared to be home. Could I knock on the door?

I checked around me, scanning the other houses. None of them looked familiar. But they didn't look unfamiliar, either. I should have paid more attention when I dropped her off. I studied the front of the house again, looking for clues. Her last name was Garnet. I checked the mailbox, but there was no name on it. I glanced around to see if any neighbors were watching, and then opened it. There was a flyer inside, from a supermarket. It was addressed to RESIDENT, which didn't help.

Then a car came around the corner. I slid the flyer back in and discreetly closed the mailbox. Then I casually walked on, my heart racing in my chest.

And then my mom called.

This was the next day, at the end of my shift. I was in the storage room, putting my Happy Bubble shirt back on its hanger, when my phone lit up.

I didn't know why she would be calling. She didn't generally talk to me directly; usually I heard stuff through my dad. But there it was: her famous name on my phone screen.

I took the call and held the phone to my ear. "Hello?"

"Hi, Nick, it's your mother."

"Hi, Mom."

She took a long breath, like this was going to be a hard conversation for her. "How are you?" she said. "How are things in Seaside?"

"Things are good," I said.

"Where are you?"

"Right now? I'm at the car wash. I'm just getting off work."

"That's right. You're working for your uncle Rob."

"Yup," I said.

"How is that?"

"It's okay. It was cloudy today. So there weren't many customers."

"I always wondered how a car wash could stay in business in a place where it rains so much."

"Well it does stay in business," I said. "And it does pretty well."

"I guess that's nice for your aunt and uncle."

"Yes. Yes, it is."

My mother took another breath. I could feel her anxiety. "There's something I need to talk to you about."

I sat down and prepared myself. Whatever this was, it wasn't going to be good.

"I'm going to be moving out of the house," she said.

"Out of our house . . . ?"

"Yes. I'm getting an apartment, closer to campus."

"We practically live on campus," I said. "How much closer can you get?"

"It's not the distance. It's the logistics of it. Your father and I . . ." She sighed. "We've discussed it, and we think it's for the best."

I said nothing. Now it was my turn to take a long breath. The truth was, it never felt right at home when it was just my dad and me. Not that my dad did anything wrong. Or that I enjoyed dealing with my mom. It was just the basic mechanics of the thing. Two guys, living together . . . something was missing. It didn't feel like a family. I don't know why. You needed a woman there, I guess. Women were what families were built around.

"So I've rented a place," continued my mother. "I think it will make things easier for everyone."

"It's not going to make things easier for me," I said. My voice cracked slightly as I said this.

"Why do you say that? How is this going to affect you?"

"Are you serious?" I said. "Are you seriously asking me that?"

"Well you seemed to do all right for the three months I was in treatment. You seemed much happier, according to your father."

"Of course we were happier," I said. "Because you weren't driving us crazy."

My mother made an annoyed sound. "Well, now I *won't* be driving you crazy. Since that's all I'm good for. Apparently."

I sat there. I could feel tears coming into my eyes.

"That's not all you're good for," I had to say. "Obviously."

"I don't want to argue about it," said my mother. "Both your father and I think this is the best solution. So that's what we're doing. I'll be moving my things next week. You can come see the apartment when you get home. When are you coming home?"

"At the end of the summer."

"Okay then, at the end of the summer. And you will always be welcome. This isn't a legal situation, so there won't be a specific custody arrangement. You're father and I are on the same page about this."

"So where am I going to be?"

"With your father, of course."

"So you just want to get rid of us. . . ."

"I never said that."

"And where will Richard be?"

"Richard? Richard has nothing to do with this."

"I bet he *does* have something to do with it. I bet he has *a lot* to do with it."

"You have no right to accuse me of anything regarding Richard. That part of my life is none of your business."

"No. You're wrong. It's totally my business. Dr. Snow even said so."

"*Dr. Snow* . . . ," said my mother dismissively. "What does he know about my relationships with my colleagues?"

"Richard's not your colleague. He's your boyfriend! And you're probably moving in with him. Because that's what you do. That's what you always do. When you get bored with people, you toss them aside. And if anyone says anything, you act superior and above it all, until you win and get what you want!"

My mother responded with icy calm: "I don't understand why you need to express this anger now, when I'm trying to have an adult conversation with you. Your father was just telling me how much improvement you've made with your attitude. And how grown-up you've become. And mature. And now you're acting like a child again, accusing me of terrible, irrational things. I don't even know how to respond to this."

Sobs began to leak out of me. "You always win, Mom. You always get exactly what you want. You know what Dr. Snow says? He says the sickest people always win. And that's you. You're the sickest person because you don't care what you do to people. All you care about is yourself."

"I'm very sorry you're so upset, Nicholas," said my mother. "But I don't think I can continue this conversation if you're going to lie about my motives and say the most hurtful things you can think of. You don't even sound like yourself. You sound like a crazy person."

"Okay, then," I said. "Hang up on me. Hang up on your only child and then go move in with your creepy boyfriend. And maybe have a couple drinks to celebrate!"

"You would like that, wouldn't you?" she said. Now she had emotion in her voice. Now she sounded on the brink of tears. "After all I've done for you! You would like to see me fail. After all the struggles I've been through, and how hard I've tried with you and your father. And now you're attacking me, saying anything you can to hurt me—"

I hung up. I had to hang up, or I was going to slam my

phone into the concrete floor. I needed my phone. I had done that in the past with my mother, destroyed things after our little talks. I couldn't destroy my phone. I needed my phone. I held it. I gripped it. *Don't hurt your phone*, I told myself. *Don't hurt your phone.*

I walked out of the Happy Bubble. I didn't know where I was going. I crossed the street and walked in the direction of the beach. My brain was overloaded, and my chest hurt. Had I lost my mother forever by being so hard on her? Or had I already lost her anyway to Richard? Or had I never actually had a mother during any of this? And what was my father going to say when he heard about my outburst? Because my mother would tell him and probably accuse him of instigating it.

My father would be pissed anyway. He believed in never losing your temper with Mom. He never did what I had just done. Except for the night he punched Richard in the face, in the front yard, but that was different—that was Richard, not her.

I walked. I continued along Broadway toward the

ocean. There were people on the sidewalks and walking along the street. Tourists. Couples. Families with kids. My mother often joked about big families at her dinner parties: how one kid was enough. She wouldn't be fooled twice. Kids! From the moment they appeared, *you* worked for *them*!

I wanted to get drunk, I realized. I went into the little store that Justin got his beer from. But I didn't know them, and they didn't know me. They weren't going to sell me anything. I left.

I was two blocks from the beach when I took a right on the little side street that cut between the hotels. At the end of this street was the tiny Seaside Library.

I'd found the library before, but it hadn't been open. Today it was. I tried to see through the window. Was Jace there? I cautiously opened the door. There she was, standing along one wall, putting some books away.

She turned and saw me. She smiled at first, but then her expression changed when she saw my face.

"Hey," she said.

"Hi," I mumbled.

"What's up?"

It was hard to speak. I wasn't sure why I'd come. "I got off work early," I managed to say.

She watched me carefully. "Are you okay?" she asked.

"Yeah," I said, avoiding her gaze. "I just got a weird phone call."

"From who?"

"From my mom," I said. "She's moving out of our house."

"Oh, I'm sorry."

"It doesn't matter. I knew she would. Better now, while I'm not there."

Jace swallowed. I could see her neck swallow because she was taller than me.

"If you can wait a few minutes, I'm just closing up. We could go somewhere."

"Yeah," I said, still looking around in an evasive way. "That would be good. Thanks."

We walked down to the Promenade. It felt good to be moving and to be outside. But in another way, it made it worse. Being in the open air, in public, I felt like I might totally disintegrate if I thought the wrong thought or said the wrong words.

We ended up on the north end of the Promenade and sat on a bench. Now I was thinking about my dad. He wasn't going to like that I'd lost my temper. He'd want me to talk to Dr. Snow. And my mom, she would use this against me. And then she'd force me to come to her house. And Richard. What was I going to do with him? I was going to fuck up his car, was my first thought. Baseball bat to the side mirrors. Baseball bat to the rear taillights. Baseball bat to the side of his balding head. But no, I wasn't going to do that. I wasn't going to do anything. I was going to get a grip on myself, that's what I was going to do.

Jace must have sensed something, because she reached over and put her hand on my hand. But that felt weird to both of us so she took it off.

"I don't know what's happening to me," I said in a low voice. I was staring at the ground. I couldn't seem to control my thoughts or what came out of my mouth.

"You're going through some things," said Jace. "This is hard. This is your *mom*."

"I feel like this is changing me," I said. "And not in a good way. I don't want to be like this. I don't want to become this person. . . ." And then I started crying. Like I burst into tears. Right there in front of Jace. God, it was terrible. It was the most embarrassing thing I'd done in my life.

I pulled myself together. I hardened my face. "Jesus, look at me," I said, wiping my tears away. "I'm totally losing it. Sorry."

"It's okay," she said. She put her hand on my shoulder. "It's totally okay."

My dad called later. It was after dinner. I was down in the basement, lying on my bed. I'd opened the back door so I could hear the trees outside, and the hoot owls, and the wind.

"Hey, kiddo," he said.

"Hey, Dad," I said.

"How're you doing?"

"I'm doing all right."

There was a pause. "So you talked to your mom."

"Yeah," I said, putting my hand over my eyes.

"She said you guys had a little dustup."

"Yeah, we did."

"She told you she's moving out."

"Yeah."

"Looks like it'll just be me here, until you get back."

I hadn't thought of that. What it would be like for my dad, sitting in that house alone. He sure got screwed in all of this. He got it worse than anybody.

"Dad?" I said.

"Yeah?"

"Did you ever love Mom?"

"Of course I did. I still do."

"Like right now you do?"

"Yes. Don't you?"

"I don't think so."

"Yes you do. She's your mother. The problem is, she has a disease. She has the disease of alcoholism. She didn't choose to have it. She didn't want her life to be like this."

"Are you sure about that? Cuz it seems to me—"

"Yes. I *am* sure of it. I'm totally sure of it. You think she wanted this to happen? You think she wants to hurt her own family? Trust me. She doesn't. This was never part of the plan."

"I guess it wouldn't be."

"That's how it goes sometimes. You can't control things. You get married. You don't know what's going to happen. In her case, she wanted a family. She wanted to have that kind of love in her life. But it's the nature of addiction. She can't always control certain things. And she self-destructs. And sometimes she hurts the people around her as a result."

I didn't say anything. I thought, *My poor dad.*

"Are you going to get a divorce?" I said.

"I don't know."

"Do you want to?

"That's something I have to work out."

"What about Richard?"

"What about him?"

"Don't you want to kill him?"

There was a brief silence. "No," said my dad in a low voice. "I don't want to kill anyone."

Neither of us talked for a while. I didn't know what to say. Neither did he.

"How's the car wash?" he finally asked me.

"It's good."

"Are you're having a good summer?"

"Yeah, I'd say so. It's been interesting. It's been a learning experience."

"Yeah?" he said. "What have you learned?"

I thought for a moment. "Actually, you don't want to know."

"That bad, huh?" said my dad. "Well try to make it back in one piece. I need some company."

"Okay, Dad. I'll try."

I went back upstairs and watched TV with Emily, Uncle Rob, and Aunt Judy. I'd already told Aunt Judy about my mom moving out. I assumed she'd told everyone else.

Nobody talked when I sat down. It occurred to me that the Reillys probably knew how my mother made fun of them. They probably hated her. But they were too polite to say anything. It was amazing sometimes, the things people managed not to say. While someone like my mom, she said whatever she felt like.

Eventually Uncle Rob and Aunt Judy went upstairs. Emily and I sat on the couch and watched *The Real Housewives of Orange County*. I figured she'd probably talked to Jace. I kind of didn't care who knew what by this time. I felt numb, which was good in a way. I thought about my dad, though. That was the saddest part. I had one more year and I was free of this mess. He'd been stuck with my mom for years. And he still was.

"Jace said you came to the library," said Emily during a commercial.

I glanced once across the couch at her. "Yeah."

Emily stared at the TV. "She still likes you, you know."

"Who does?" I said.

"Jace."

That seemed like a weird thing to bring up at that moment.

"I mean, I know you have a lot going on," said Emily. "But she does."

"Well I like her, too."

"Do you?"

"Yes," I said.

"It doesn't seem like it."

"Well what do you want me to do exactly?" I said back.

"I don't know," said Emily. "Act like it? Tell her? Talk to her?"

"It's not like my life is going super smoothly at the moment," I said, staring hard at the TV.

Emily said nothing. She could really be annoying with her rules about what boys were supposed to do. Especially since she was the only one who knew what they were.

"She knows I like her," I said.

"Girls never know for sure," said Emily. "Unless you tell them."

That was it. That made me mad "Well what if we're just friends? Okay? How about that?"

"Is that how you feel?"

"Yes. That's how I feel."

"Then tell her."

"I don't have to tell her. She knows. She said it herself."

Emily stared at the TV.

"Everything is fine between Jace and me. And in the meantime, how about everybody just chills out and gives me a few seconds to figure my own stuff out? How about that?"

"Don't get mad at me. I'm trying to help you."

I sunk back into the couch. It was true. I had no right to get mad at Emily. Or maybe I did have a right. I didn't know.

I didn't know anything by that point.

PART THREE

AUGUST

During the first week of August there were three ninety-
five degree days in a row, which had never happened before
in Seaside. Everyone was talking about it. The thing I
noticed was that everything actually dried out. Like stuff
that had probably never been dry, in this soggy, drizzly,
town. And then a hot, dusty wind began to blow down off
the mountains, and you felt like the whole town might
catch fire, which turned out to be a real danger, according
to the constant radio and TV announcements.

The third day of the heat wave was the busiest at the
car wash. The tunnel ran nonstop. Justin and I barely got a
break from the vacuuming. Mike was so busy, he couldn't
get in a smoke break and I had to take over for him while he
sucked down a couple cigarettes in the back.

The heat made people cranky too. Some guy from

Las Vegas started yelling at me for spilling a Coke on his new car's carpet. Never mind that the Coke can was rolling around on the floor when he drove in. Justin started arguing with him while I stood by. Mike finally came over and growled at him to shut up. Then Kyle hurried over and apologized and comped the guy a free car wash and carpet shampoo, which, fortunately, he didn't have time to get.

And then later, just before closing, a little kid somehow wandered into the tunnel. Everyone freaked out, and Justin dove for the kill switch, which shut the whole thing down, possibly saving the kid's life. The mother nearly had a heart attack, and while everyone was trying to calm her down, her little dog escaped from their car and almost got hit by a log truck on the highway.

Meanwhile, I was still thinking about my mother and our phone call. I hadn't heard anything back from her. Sooner or later I would. You didn't just hang up on my mother and get away with it. Somehow, some way, she would get back at you.

Justin and I walked into town after work. I'd managed to not mention my family stuff to him, but once we were away from the Happy Bubble, I couldn't seem to help myself.

"My mom and dad are splitting up," I said.

"No shit?" he said. "When did that happen."

"Couple days ago."

"Ah, man," he said. "That's too bad. Sorry to hear that."

"Yeah," I said. "I kinda expected it. I just didn't know when exactly it would happen."

We made our way along the crowded sidewalk. The record heat had brought record amounts of tourists.

"You wanna get a bottle?" asked Justin.

"Nah, I'm good."

"You sure?" he said. "It cures what ails ya."

"Yeah?"

"You know it does."

I kinda did want to chill out. "Yeah, okay," I said.

Justin cut cross the street and angled toward the little store where they sold him liquor. I waited outside, as usual.

When he came back out, I said, "Would you mind if we didn't sit under the stairs?"

"What's wrong with under the stairs?"

I shrugged. "It just kinda feels like . . ."

"Like what?" he asked. He genuinely didn't know.

"It feels like something a bum would do."

Justin stopped. He looked at me. It was kind of a weird moment. But then he started to nod. "Okay," he said. "Okay."

"I mean, no offense—"

"No, no, I feel you," said Justin. "I can see what you're saying." He thought about it more. He stopped walking. "You know what?"

"What?" I said.

"I'll get us some Coke cups. And we'll put the whiskey in there. And make whiskey and Cokes. How's that?"

"That sounds good."

"And that way we can sit wherever we want. We can sit on the Promenade. And we won't look like bums."

An hour later we were sprawled on one of the benches in front of the Del Mar Hotel. The whiskey and Cokes we were drinking, hidden inside ordinary Coke cups, tasted sweet and delicious.

"So what's going on with your parents?" Justin asked me.

"My mom's moving out," I said. "So she can be with her boyfriend."

Justin shook his head. "People . . . ," he said. "They're always up to something."

"My dad says it's because she's an alcoholic. But I think she just doesn't give a shit."

"Yeah," said Justin. "Probably both."

The sun had set and the beach was going dark. Tourists and beach walkers were coming in, climbing up the stairs from the sand to the Promenade.

"I only got one more year at home anyway," I said. I sipped some of my drink through the straw. The alcohol hit you harder through a straw, I was noticing. I was pretty drunk.

"You goin' off to college?" asked Justin.

"Yeah," I said, a little embarrassed.

"*College* . . . ," said Justin, thinking about it. "Don't know much about that. Seems like it could be pretty fun, though. If you're suited to it."

"Yeah, I *am* sort of suited to it. I actually *like* to study. I'm good at it."

Justin smiled and nodded to himself. "I bet you are," he rasped. "I bet you are."

It was totally dark when we got off our bench and tossed our cups in the trash. There were still people on the main beach, standing around their beach fires. Justin was drunker than I was, or he should have been; he'd been adding extra whiskey to his cup all the time we'd been sitting there. But I was definitely feeling no pain. And my family problems? They were still there, I knew that. They were just further away now. I was seeing them from a new perspective. I looked around, at the people on the beach, at the people walking their dogs. *Everyone has problems,* I told myself. *The world is full of problems.*

And that's when I saw the four guys coming up the Promenade.

They were the guys from the Fourth of July, the guys
Justin and his buddies had beaten up. One of them had two
white bandages on his face. Another was carrying a hammer.
By the grim, determined looks on their faces, it was clear
they were looking for someone. They were looking for us.

"Uh-oh," I said.

"Is that . . . ?" asked Justin.

"I think it is . . . ," I said back. "What should we do?"

"Uh . . . run?"

Run, yeah, but where? In our drunkenness, the first
thing we did was knock into each other. Then I turned and
started jogging north, up the Promenade. Justin went the
other way, running toward the stone railing of the circular
viewing area. *What is he doing?* I wondered.

The four of them had spotted us by now and broke into

a run. At first, they ignored me and zeroed in on Justin. Without panicking, Justin ran casually to the railing and vaulted over it. It was a pretty far drop to the sand below. Ten, twelve feet maybe. When the prep guys got to it, they stopped and looked down. None of them wanted to jump. Two of them broke off and ran around to the stairs. And then the other two turned and ran after me.

Jesus Christ, I thought. I had slowed down to see what would happen to Justin. Now I turned and ran hard up the Promenade. I looked back after a few seconds. My two pursuers were keeping up. They were staying right with me. They were probably athletes of some kind. I felt a surge of hatred for their rich-kid haircuts and polo shirts as I pushed myself to top speed. But truthfully I probably had more in common with them than I did Justin.

I ran as fast as I could, then cut right, down a side street. Thank God I knew where I was going. I ran one short block, turned left, ran down an alley, turned right, and then ducked into the driveway of an old garage. I immediately crouched down behind a pickup truck and tried to catch my breath.

It appeared I had momentarily lost them. I wondered if I should try to call someone for backup. I had Tyler's number. And Kyle's. I reached into my pants pocket for my phone.

But at that moment I heard footsteps, and, out of nowhere, here came the prep dudes from the other direction. They totally saw me.

I jumped to my feet and ran. I got on Belmont Street and sprinted with everything I had toward the highway five blocks away. There was a gas station there and a convenience store. Hopefully they wouldn't do anything if I could make it to a public place.

But then a car came ripping around a corner. It was a Jeep. It was coming right at me and I had to throw myself out of the way. I just happened to glance up to see Nicole and Phoebe staring at me in disbelief. They drove by without slowing down. *I should have waved for them to stop!* But now they were gone, and I still had four long blocks to run to the highway. I scrambled to my feet and started running again. It was hard going now. I was exhausted. And drunk. One of the prep guys was catching up to me, and he was the one with the hammer.

When I couldn't run anymore, I turned and faced him. "Dude," I gasped. "No *hammers* . . . seriously . . . that's assault . . . with a deadly weapon. . . . They'll send you to prison. . . ."

The guy stopped running too. He was as gassed as I was. And I guess he believed me about the hammer, because he looked at it once and then tossed it into the street. What did he need a hammer for? He was already bigger than me. And his buddy was right behind him.

I was still back-pedaling away from the two of them. "Dudes," I said to them. "Nobody needs to get hurt here." I was totally out of breath. And so were they. But they were still advancing on me, still calculating how to take me down. Finally they charged. I turned and ran, but I had no chance. They caught me easily. One jumped on my back. I managed to stay on my feet for a few more steps, and then the other one jumped on too. We all went down, me first, with the two of them on top of me. The impact with the street was brutal. I was knocked out and lost track of everything, so much so that I didn't see the Jeep or the girls or whatever happened next.

A moment later, though, the prep guys were scrambling to get off me. I looked up and saw Phoebe standing over us. She had picked up the hammer and was hitting the guys with it. Like really pounding on them. Both of the preps rolled off me and scurried away as fast as they could. Then one of them turned back toward her, thinking he could get the hammer back. And that's when Nicole maced them both.

"*Ahhhhhhh!*" screamed the guy who got the first liquid blast in the face. The other guy ducked and ran, avoiding the liquid stream and escaping down the street. His screaming friend followed.

I stared up at Phoebe in amazement. I couldn't believe I'd escaped. I was about to get the living shit beat out of me, and now I was saved!

I sat up. I moved my head around. I checked my hands and flexed my various body parts. I was pretty banged up, but I hadn't broken anything. My pants were ripped, and my shirt was dirty, but I was otherwise in one piece. My cheek, though, I suddenly felt it. It had scraped against the concrete. It began to burn and sting. I touched it. It felt like it was on fire.

I looked over and saw that Nicole was calling someone on her phone. Phoebe was standing in the street, looking at the hammer.

"This is a nice hammer," she said.

"What kind is it?" said Nicole with her phone to her face.

"Stanley."

"Those are good," said Nicole.

"Who are you calling?" I asked Nicole. I was still out of breath, I realized when I spoke.

"The police," she said.

"That might not be the best idea," I said. "We actually beat up one of their guys first."

Nicole looked at her nails. "Doesn't matter," she said. "You're from here and they're not. So they'll get arrested, and their parents will pay a fine. The police need the money."

My cheek was really burning now. I touched it with my fingers. "Okay," I said. "If that's how you do it."

"That's how we do it," said Nicole.

31

Nicole decided we should go to Phoebe's, since it was nearby and there was beer there. The house we pulled into looked different from the house I remembered. But it was night now, and the situation had changed a lot.

I crawled out of the Jeep, in some pain, and followed Nicole and Phoebe inside. It was totally dark. Phoebe turned on the lights.

We went into the kitchen. There was a small table and some chairs. The counter was messy with dirty dishes and empty beer cans.

Nicole lit a cigarette and looked at her phone. I was touching my face, which stung terribly.

"That doesn't look good," said Nicole, meaning my face.

Phoebe stepped closer to me. She pulled my hand away and studied my cheek. She was shorter than me, so she had to tilt her head up slightly to look. The angle made her face look even more alluring than usual.

She pointed to a chair and motioned for me to sit. I did as I was instructed. "Yeah, the reason those guys were after me . . . ," I began, assuming Nicole and Phoebe would want to hear the whole story. But neither of them were listening.

Phoebe sat down next to me and inspected my street-burned cheek. I could feel her tiny fingertips touching the ripped-up skin. "We should clean this," she said.

Nicole, meanwhile, went to the refrigerator and got three beers. She set one on the table next to Phoebe, one next to me, and opened one for herself.

The kitchen went silent. Phoebe sat back in her chair and lit a cigarette of her own. She took a long swig from her beer.

I held the cold beer against my burning face, which made it feel better. "Do you live here by yourself?" I asked Phoebe.

"With my mom," she said, flicking ash into an ashtray. "But she always stays at her boyfriend's."

I nodded. "My mother has a boyfriend," I said.

Phoebe drank more beer and then put her cigarette out. Then she went into the bathroom and came back with a bottle of rubbing alcohol. She poured some onto a dish towel and began dabbing the side of my face. The alcohol stung so bad my eyes watered. But I endured it. I enjoyed it. I liked that Phoebe was touching me. I didn't want her to stop.

"I wonder if those guys got away," Nicole asked, looking at her phone. "I wonder if they'll want their hammer back."

"It's my hammer now," said Phoebe.

After she'd finished cleaning my cheek, Phoebe disappeared somewhere and then returned with a pair of tweezers. She showed them to me. "There's a tiny little rock stuck in your face," she said. "Do you want me to take it out?"

I didn't want to look cowardly, so I nodded. Phoebe gripped my skull and tilted my head to one side, considering how best to remove the tiny rock. I enjoyed this, too. I liked how Phoebe moved my head around. I could feel her breath on the side of my face. Then she stabbed the tweezers into my face, which hurt more than the rubbing alcohol.

"Ouch!" I said, jerking my head away.

"Maybe you should use a needle," said Nicole.

"No," said Phoebe, standing now. She held my head tightly against her body and gouged me a second time with the tweezers. "I think . . . I almost . . . *there*! I got it!"

She was going to show me the rock, but it fell on the floor. We both looked down like we might see it, but the floor was pretty dirty.

Phoebe sat back down and drank some more of her beer. I held my cold beer bottle against my aching face.

Nicole's phone made a ding, and she checked her messages. "That's Connor," she said. "I gotta go."

"Who's Connor?" I asked, but nobody answered.

Nicole downed the rest of her beer and started gathering

her things. I started to stand up too, thinking she could drop me off somewhere.

But Nicole shook her head. "I can't give you a ride."

"Oh . . . ," I said.

"You can hang out here if you want," said Phoebe. "For a little while."

"I gotta go," said Nicole, leaving us to figure it out. She marched to the front door. "Bye!" she called.

"Bye!" said Phoebe.

When Nicole was gone, it was just Phoebe and me. This was pretty much the exact situation I'd been dreaming about. Now if I could just not blow it. I decided to keep my mouth shut as much as possible. That had worked before.

Phoebe seemed a bit nervous herself. She cleaned up a little in the kitchen, putting away the beer bottles and taking out the trash. Eventually, she returned to the table and sat down across from me. She drank more beer. She lit another cigarette. She watched me. There was that same strange quality in her eyes, like she wasn't quite seeing me. Maybe she was thinking about something else.

When her beer was gone, she put the bottle in the sink. "You wanna see the family business?" she asked me.

"Sure," I said.

She took me into the back of the house, into an enclosed porch area that had been walled off and turned into a work space. There were two long tables, a heat-press machine, and a dozen large boxes stacked up along one wall. The boxes were full of different colored T-shirts. That's what Phoebe and her mother did to make money: They made T-shirts that said SEASIDE on them or CHILL ZONE or LIFE'S A BEACH or I WENT TO SEASIDE AND ALL I GOT WAS THIS LOUSY T-SHIRT. The heat-press machine stamped these slogans onto T-shirts or hoodies. Phoebe and her mother also ironed patches onto the front of trucker hats: pot leaves or silhouettes of naked women or the word SEASIDE or 420.

"And you sell these?" I said.

"Of course we sell them," said Phoebe. "What else would we do with them?"

"I don't know."

"Here, I'll show you." She took a yellow T-shirt out of a box and unfolded it. Then she moved to the heat-press machine: "The way it works is . . . you push this button here . . . and then you wait for the press to heat up. . . ." She gave me a cute *waiting* look. "Then, when it's nice and hot . . . and the green light turns on . . . you put the T-shirt in here, like this. . . ." She slid the T-shirt expertly into the machine and aligned it perfectly on the first try. "Then you put the press down on top of it . . . like that. . . . Do you smell that burning smell? That means it's working." She gave me a sarcastic smile, like wasn't this the funnest thing ever? "Then you wait a few seconds . . . and then you lift it back up . . . and there you have it! A stupid T-shirt, perfect for friends and family!" She held it out for me to see.

I smiled. I laughed. The T-shirt said, CHILL ZONE. I said:

"That is the greatest Chill Zone T-shirt I have ever seen."

She stopped then and looked closer at my face. "Oh, I forgot to put a Band-Aid on your cheek!"

I followed her back into the main part of the house. She went into the bathroom to find a Band-Aid. "Come in here," she said.

I squeezed into the small bathroom and stood behind her as she dug through the medicine cabinet.

When she found a large, square Band-Aid, she made me sit on the toilet seat. Before she unwrapped the Band-Aid, she wanted to dab at my face again with the rubbing alcohol. This time, in the cramped space of the bathroom, she put her hand on my shoulder. Then she gripped my chin. Her stomach was also touching me quite a bit. And the front of her thighs. At one point she looked deep into my eyes, then looked away.

She unwrapped the Band-Aid and peeled away the backing. She bent closer, her face right next to mine. Slowly, carefully, she positioned the square patch on my cheek and then pressed it into place.

When it was done, she smiled at me. She casually ran her hand through my hair. Then she moved my knees together so she could sit on my lap.

"Do you mind?" she said, lowering herself onto me.

"No," I said.

She smiled again and settled her weight on my thighs. I wasn't sure what she was doing, but I played along, putting one hand on her back and the other on her knee. She in

Some time later I woke up in Phoebe's bed. I wasn't sure how much time had passed. I turned my head, and Phoebe was lying beside me, on her back, naked. She was holding her phone, her face lit up in the darkness. The sheet was covering most of her, but her pale white shoulders were exposed and glowed in the screen light.

"Finally," she said. "You're awake."

"Yeah," I said, enjoying the happy numbness that filled my body.

She studied her phone. "You were snoring."

"I was?" I said.

She nodded.

"But I don't snore."

"Nobody thinks they snore," she said. I was surprised by the flat tone in her voice. But I was too blissed out to care.

turn began to play with my hair, combing it with her fingers first to the right and then to the left.

"I like your hair," she said. "Nice and thick."

"I like your hair too," I said. She was sitting on my lap, so my eyes were even with her shoulders and chest. So now it was me, looking up at her. And with the bright bathroom light, I could really see every detail of her face. She looked both beautiful and harsh, somehow.

She stopped playing with my hair and let her hand rest on my shoulder. Her expression grew serious. She began to stare at my mouth. I stared at hers. She bent closer and touched her lips to mine.

The kiss was more controlled this time. It didn't have the random, casual quality like at the party. It was a deeper, slower, more deliberate. It felt very adult to me, very sophisticated. I slipped my hands around her waist and pulled her small body tight against mine. Something began to happen, a craving, an uncontrollable desire. The more we touched, the more we *had* to touch. I lifted her up and repositioned her, so she was straddling me, so I could press her against me completely. In that moment a kind of current seemed to flow between us. It felt electric, euphoric, supercharged with feeling. Whatever it was, I couldn't get enough of it. I felt like I would die if we were separated.

The four seconds it took for us to move to her bedroom seemed like an eternity apart.

"You should probably go," she said.

"What time is it?" I said.

She didn't answer.

I lifted my head and looked at the clock radio beside the bed. It was one fifteen a.m. I did need to go. But the thought of getting out of that bed filled me with dread. I didn't want to be separated from Phoebe.

I settled my head back down. *Just a few more minutes,* I thought. She continued to stare into the soft light of her phone. It was odd how blank her face was. Wasn't she happy about what had just happened?

"You're sure you want me to go?" I said.

She nodded her head yes. Which didn't feel so great. But she probably had her reasons.

So I did it. I forced myself to a sitting position. I swung my legs out of the bed and stood. I untangled my ripped Dickies and put them on. I slipped on my Happy Bubble shirt. Phoebe hadn't moved. She typed something into her phone with her thumbs.

"Who are you texting?" I asked.

Phoebe didn't answer. I buttoned my shirt. I felt my cheek. The Band-Aid was still there. It didn't hurt as bad as it had before. "Hey, thanks for patching me up," I said.

"You're welcome," she said, without looking up.

"Okay," I said, when I had all my clothes on. "I guess I'll go."

She finally glanced once in my direction. "Give me a kiss?" she said.

"I thought you'd never ask," I said, grinning. I lay across the bed and touched her hair and kissed her lips. It was an amazing kiss. All of Phoebe's kisses were amazing. So warm and soft, but also with just the right amount of pressure and never trying too hard or going too fast, just perfectly relaxed, and in her slow, sensual rhythm.

"You're really good at that," I whispered, brushing her hair away from her face with my fingers.

When she didn't respond, I lifted myself off the bed. I stood and watched her for another few seconds. She shut off her phone and set it down on the table beside her. "Bye," she said.

"Bye," I said back. I turned and walked through the kitchen. I opened the front door and went outside.

The air was colder than I was expecting. Low clouds had rolled in, and a light mist was visible in the one streetlamp on the block.

As I walked down the driveway, my head began to hurt. And my bruised knee made each step painful. Phoebe's presence had made me forget my injuries, but now that I was alone, I could feel myself again. I hobbled into the street and limped along as best I could. The misty wetness swirled in the streetlight. You could see the actual water particles. *What a strange and mysterious world*, I thought. And at its center was a person I was now joined with forever. Phoebe. Phoebe Garnet. I was in love with the most extraordinary girl I'd ever known. It was like I had entered a new phase of my life. The phase where my dreams came true. Where the impossible was possible. Where a guy like me got a girl like that.

I couldn't move very fast. Every part of me hurt. It took me ten minutes to get to the highway.

There weren't many cars out at that hour. As I stood at the intersection, an oversized pickup truck turned toward me off the highway and rumbled down Phoebe's street. I could see the driver in his cab, a big, burly guy in a baseball cap. I continued to watch the truck as it slowed for the individual stop signs.

I went back to watching the traffic light. When the WALK sign came on, I limped across the highway and began the two-mile hike back to the Reillys'. It took a while, but I made it, and when I got to the basement door, I paused for a moment. I turned and looked into the dark, silent forest behind the house. I would remember this night for the rest of my life, I knew. I already loved Phoebe in a way I didn't know was possible. More than Kate even. More than anyone.

And it had only just begun.

Justin was at work the next day, without a scratch on him.
He'd escaped the prep guys by locking himself in the maintenance room next to the bathrooms under the Promenade. Being tourists, they couldn't find him at first, and when they did, they couldn't get him out. They pounded on the thick metal door, but Justin just sat there patiently, playing solitaire on his phone with his three fingers like he does.

I gave him a short version of what happened to me—leaving out the part about being with Phoebe. I'm not sure why I didn't tell him that. I guess I was afraid it would ruin it somehow, or he might tell me something I didn't want to hear. He had acted so lukewarm about her the night of the Fourth of July party.

Anyway, there was no time to talk. We had a million customers that day. We ran around vacuuming and windexing.

Needless to say, I kept seeing Phoebe in my mind, not an exact picture, more like a pale blur of softness and warmth, the feeling of being so close to someone, so connected, so entwined. Like the morning I found her on the beach, there was a vague feeling of unreality to it all. Like had I really been there? In her bed? Had that part really happened? But it had. I knew it had. I could still feel it in my body. I could still smell it on my skin. Phoebe was all over me.

I thought about her life, making her T-shirts and being so cute and being in love with me (I hoped) and me being in love with her (totally). I wondered if she could teach me how to make T-shirts. I'd rather do that than vacuum. Maybe I could live with her for the rest of the summer, and help her and her mother with their business. But no, that wasn't realistic. That was too much. I had to be careful with Phoebe. She wasn't going to tolerate too much mushy stuff, or me trying too hard to involve myself in her life.

So I went back to remembering how she smelled, the taste of her neck and her lips, the feel of her bare skin under my fingers. And how she touched me and how I touched her. And how her eyes looked when we were pressed together, so intense and quiet and whispery in her bed.

I imagined going to her house some morning. I would sit in her work space, leaning back in a chair and drinking coffee, while she made trucker hats and told me about her life. Outside the birds would chirp; the sun would shine. Maybe I could think up some new slogans for her T-shirts, something better than "Life's A Beach." Then later, at night, we'd drink wine in her kitchen and talk, and she'd smoke cigarettes in her sexy way, though of course I would need to work on her about her smoking. I mean, it looks cool, but it's terrible for you and gives you cancer. Phoebe getting cancer, that would kill me. I couldn't even let the thought into my mind. Instead, I pictured Phoebe in her workroom, surrounded by her T-shirt boxes, gliding from table to table and saying odd, sarcastic things. She always put up this bored exterior, but you knew some inner part of her was happier than that. How else could she be so cute, so funny, so sexy? She was like a child, in a way, innocent and yet not innocent, but still smart enough to keep the world at a distance. That was the part that really drew you in. Her separateness. That elusive, unknowable quality. What did she think of me? What did she think of anything? It was a mystery. A mystery you wanted to crawl inside of and be ecstatically confused by for the rest of your life.

When I got off work, I didn't feel like being around people, so I slipped out right at six and walked to the beach. I didn't have Phoebe's phone number. That was weird. How did I forget to ask for her phone number? And why hadn't she offered it?

Another thing was Nicole. If Phoebe became my girlfriend, I would be hanging out with Nicole a lot too. Which was fine. The three of us would do things, drive places in their Jeep, though to be honest, the Jeep seemed a little unsafe. And Nicole's driving, it didn't exactly inspire confidence. But I did like how Nicole took charge of things. And her attitude in general: yakking and loud and funny . . . and sexy when she wanted to be . . . and a holy terror at other times.

But back to Phoebe: Hopefully, we'd spend most of our time alone. We'd go for walks on the beach, a blanket over our shoulders. I would put my arm around her waist and smell her hair and tell her about my life in Eugene. Maybe she would want to visit me there once school started. She could hang out at my dad's house—there was plenty of space; we had two empty bedrooms now. What if she wanted to come live with us? She totally could. *And she could go to college.* Oh my God, why hadn't I thought of that before? She could come live with us, and she could go to school and learn about clothes or fashion or whatever. Because that was another thing about Phoebe: She always looked fantastic. From the moment I first saw her, my eye always went to her first, not Nicole, who dressed in obvious party-girl clothes that any Seaside girl might wear. Phoebe actually had a style all her own. And the way she moved, like when she was dabbing my face with the alcohol, there was that super-cute, girlish quality to her gestures. And how incredible it felt to be the receiver of those gestures. Like in the bathroom, when she put the Band-Aid on my face and then touched my shoulder and my neck and my hair. And her lips, grazing my lips, the lightest possible touch, oh my God, I couldn't think about that without my heart practi- cally exploding. And then into her room, into her bed. To be so close. To be so in love. To be *making love*. Because that's what it felt like: *making love, drowning in love, being devoured by love*. And letting yourself feel it. All of it. Letting yourself go. Losing yourself completely . . .

But yeah, anyway, thinking more practically, she probably needed help with more ordinary things. Maybe she could put her T-shirt business online. She'd probably make more money. Then she could move to Eugene. She could get her own car. The smoking and drinking so much, that was not good. But I could help her with that. Having a steady boyfriend would calm her down. I could do that. I could be that rock she needed.

I walked all the way to Gearhart, lost in my Phoebe dreams. Since I was there, I trudged up through the dunes into the town. It was August, and warm, so there were plenty of people around. The parking lot of the Pacific Grill was full, I noticed. People were driving in and out on the polished gravel. I thought about Jace and our dinner there. That was fun. I'd done a lot of fun things with Jace. And that time we kissed in her car, that had been very sweet, very high school. Maybe we'd stay in touch. I could friend her on Facebook so I could follow her progress.

And then I realized I could friend Phoebe on Facebook. I pulled out my phone and searched for her. But she didn't seem to be on there. That was odd. Who wasn't on Facebook? Nicole was, but she didn't post much, and most of her pictures were random party shots of half-naked girls falling out of cars or passed out on the stairs at some party. I kept searching Phoebe Garnet, but however I tried it, I couldn't find anything. I'd ask her about that. Why no Facebook? Wouldn't that be good advertising for her T-shirts? I'd be sure to tell her that. It seemed like she might not have the best sense for business. I could help. Maybe she could take some marketing classes, while she was living with me and my dad. . . .

I never mentioned Phoebe around Emily, or anywhere at the Reilly house. When Kyle came back from Oregon State, I considered saying something to him, but I didn't, even though it made me secretly proud to be linked to him, since he'd been with Nicole and I was now with Phoebe. Though I also knew that the reason Kyle wasn't with Nicole anymore was because she'd gone too far in the party-girl direction, while he was going the other direction.

Then one night Emily texted me that she and Jace and some other people were having a beach fire. They picked me up at work. It was getting dark now at nine instead of ten, like it had at the beginning of summer. I sat in the back seat of Jace's car while they gossiped, and I looked out the window and thought about Phoebe. At the Cove, we climbed down the trail and joined a small gathering of people who already had a fire going. Kelsey was there and Lauren, standing around with some other younger people. Emily's boyfriend, Oliver, was there, with some of his friends from Astoria.

Jace had a blanket, and I helped her lay it out. There was beer and marshmallows, and Oliver and his friends had a box of wine. So then we drank and ate potato chips out of a bag, which had somehow gotten full of sand. This time someone did have a guitar, two guitars actually, and since there were only eight of us, the whole group sang and tried to remember the words to different songs. But even then, even singing in the firelight with Jace and Emily and all these other nice people, I kept thinking about Phoebe and how I'd found her on this very beach, and when I would hopefully see her again. I wondered if she might show up here, though Emily's friends were too young for her, and too nice and too respectable. Phoebe would be bored roasting marshmallows and singing old Nirvana songs with a bunch of fifteen- and sixteen-year-olds. Or maybe she would be totally into it. That was the thing about her — you really didn't know. Which was good in a way. You could sit around and wonder about her as long as you wanted, or as long as you had time, or forever if you felt like it.

"So you're Emily's cousin?" said the guy next to me. This was Alex, one of Oliver's friends. He didn't look like a Seaside person; he had a nice haircut and an expensive shawl-style sweater like college kids wore in Eugene.

"Yeah," I said. "I've been staying with her family over the summer."

"Where you from?"

"Eugene."

"Ahhh," said Alex. "University of Oregon. That must be fun."

"It's all right," I said. "What about you?"

"Astoria. Me and Oliver drove down."

"You guys come down here a lot?"

"Oh, yeah," he said. "Seaside's more fun than Astoria. You guys have better parties than us. . . ."

"Yeah?" I said, smiling. "So Seaside's more the party town?"

"Seaside's *definitely* the party town."

I smiled and drank my beer. "Do you know Phoebe and Nicole?" I asked.

"Sure. Everyone knows them."

"Yeah? Why's that?"

He shrugged. "Just, you know . . . cuz they party. And they do crazy shit. And Nicole went out with Kyle. So everyone knows who she is."

"What about Phoebe?" I asked him.

"Phoebe? I dunno. Same thing, I guess."

"She seems quieter," I said.

"I guess so," said Alex. "I mean, I don't know either of them myself. They're just the people you hear about. The people other people talk about."

"Yeah," I said.

"I mean, Phoebe. She's supposedly . . ." His voice trailed off. Then he drank some of his beer.

I waited for him to finish his sentence. He didn't.

"She's supposedly what . . . ?" I had to ask.

"I dunno. She's like . . ." He shrugged, and then lowered his voice: "Sometimes you hear things."

"Like what?" I said.

"I dunno. Nothing in particular. Just . . . you know . . ."

"No, I don't," I said, pressing him. "What do you hear?"

But now Alex heard the urgency in my voice. He could see the intensity in my face.

So he became diplomatic.

"You just hear stuff," he said. "It's none of my business. People talk. Nicole and Kyle, when they were together, they were like 'the couple.' Every high school kid knew about them. Even in Astoria."

"But what about Phoebe?"

"Phoebe was Nicole's best friend," he said, shrugging. "Still is, as far as I know."

He was avoiding the question. I had to figure out a different way to ask it. But then I saw Jace walking toward us, which forced me to drop the subject.

35

When Jace came over, Alex left. She took his place on the blanket. She was wearing shorts, so her long white legs turned a yellowish gold in the firelight. She was also wearing Nikes. Brand new. She did that sometimes, dressed very prep, even though she actually lived in a tiny house in Seaside. It was part of her plan to escape.

"Hey," I said as she settled herself. She had an old Starbucks cup with some of Oliver's red wine in it.

"Hi," she said back.

I smiled at her. We really did like each other. That was the thing that annoyed me about Emily. Jace and I were fine. We were genuine friends.

"Have you talked to your parents any more?" she asked me.

"I talked to my dad."

"How was that?"

"Fine."

"You'll have to go back soon."

"Don't remind me," I said, sipping my beer. I stared up into the night sky and looked at the moon over Tillamook Head. I could hear the gentle rush of the ocean waves behind us. I could smell the salty tang of the sea.

"Well at least you're a senior," she said. "That'll be fun, won't it?"

"Hopefully," I said.

"I mean, family stuff," she said. "Everybody hates their family."

"Do you hate your family?"

"Sometimes," she said. "I mean, I don't *hate* them. But you know. They definitely make things difficult."

"Are you looking forward to your senior year?" I asked.

She laughed. "At our school you get senior privileges. Which means they let you drive down to the Freezie Burger at lunch. So that's a big thrill."

"Hey, I like Freezie Burger!" I said. "I wish we had a Freezie Burger near my school."

Jace smiled and drank her wine. Someone threw a large piece of driftwood into the fire, and it exploded in a cloud of sparks and glowing embers. Jace had to brush one off the shoulder of her hoodie. Another one landed in her hair, and I had to swat at it several times to get it off.

She seemed to like it when I touched her. Poor Jace. There weren't any boys for her in Seaside. Except for maybe someone like Alex. But he wouldn't appreciate her the way I did. No, I had been her best chance for a summer romance. But I had fallen for someone else.

Later the four of us, Emily and Oliver and Jace and I, went for a walk on the beach. Oliver and Emily were having a private conversation, so Jace and I lagged back. As we walked, I felt a sudden urge to tell Jace about Phoebe. I had to tell someone, at some point. I turned and looked at her. She turned toward me, too. But I couldn't say it. Because I knew it would hurt her. It was a painful moment. Maybe Emily was right; maybe I wasn't handling this correctly. But how was I supposed to handle it?

The next day, after an early shift at the car wash, I went to the coffee shop and sat in one of the cushy chairs with *Letters to a Young Poet*. But I couldn't focus. I literally could not get through the first paragraph. So I went for a walk. And as I walked, I got out my phone. I found myself calling Dr. Snow.

The receptionist put me through.

"Nick!" he said. "How are you?"

"Hi, Dr. Snow," I said.

"I'm so glad you called. How's your summer going?"

"Good. Good," I said, talking louder as I passed the bumper cars on Main Street. "I'm in Seaside. I'm staying with my aunt and uncle. I'm working at their car wash."

"Yes. I remember. And how is that?"

"It's okay. It's good. It's fun."

"And how's your mother doing?"

"She's still sober. Last I heard. Actually, she's leaving my dad. She probably already left. She's moving out."

"Oh. I didn't know that."

"Yeah. She's probably going back with that guy Richard."

"I see. Well how about you? How are you doing with everything?"

"I'm okay. It's been nice to be away. It's sort of different up here."

"In Seaside? How so?"

"People are more . . . you know, it's a small town. So it's just more . . . it's smaller."

"I see," said Dr. Snow.

"Yeah . . ."

"That sounds great, Nick. I'm so glad you're checking in. I'm sure you want to talk more about the situation with your mother. I'm looking at my schedule. I've got a cancellation at five thirty this afternoon. We could do a phone session then, if you'd like."

"Actually, there's this other thing that's happening."

"Yeah? What's that?"

"I'm in love."

"You're in love?" said Dr. Snow.

"Yeah, but I feel sort of . . . afraid of it."

"Of being in love?"

"Yeah. It's this local girl. She parties a lot. She smokes cigarettes."

"Okay."

205

"I mean, she's great," I said. "She's super fun. And kinda weird. She's got inside my brain in a way. It's hard to explain."

"Does she know how you feel about her?"

"Yeah . . . I think so. . . ."

"And does she reciprocate your feelings?"

As I thought about this, I pictured Phoebe on the beach that morning. The calm ocean, the stillness in the air. I remembered pulling the sleeping bag back and the sight of Phoebe's pale, helpless body. How I loved her in that moment. How my heart seemed to leap out of my chest.

"Nick?" said Dr. Snow. "Hello? Are you there?"

"Yeah," I said. "I'm just thinking. . . ." This happened with Dr. Snow sometimes. My thoughts would take me to a place that I couldn't bring him along. I mean, I liked Dr. Snow. And I trusted him. But he was an adult. He didn't think of love as a force that takes you over. He thought of it as "a relationship." And then he'd want to say if it was "healthy" or "unhealthy." And then he'd talk about "boundaries" or "emotional needs." He didn't know how it could get inside you and tear you up. You couldn't make it into something rational. Love was nature. It came down on you like a thundercloud, like an ocean storm. And trying to control it or manage it, you couldn't do that, you couldn't control a storm. You couldn't control the violence of the world.

"You know . . . ," I said. "I'd like to do a phone session, but I can't today."

"This sounds like something we definitely need to talk about."

"How about I'll call back tomorrow?" I said. "And figure out when the best time would be."

"Of course. Call tomorrow. Talk to Carol and set up an appointment."

"Okay, I'll do that," I said, and I hung up.

I was already walking toward the Promenade when I ended the call. Now I turned in the direction of Phoebe's.

It took about ten minutes. I didn't let myself think too much. It seemed possible that I might lose my nerve if I did. So no thinking. That was the rule I set for myself: *No thinking.*

I arrived at her house. I didn't let myself hesitate and kept right on walking, up the empty driveway and along the little path to the front door. I rang the bell, or I tried to. It didn't seem to be working. So I knocked, in a polite way, and then knocked again louder, in case she was in the work-room in the back.

A moment later I heard footsteps. My heart rose to my throat. I took a deep breath and waited.

The doorknob turned, and with some difficulty the door opened.

It was Phoebe. She was barefoot, in shorts. She looked like she'd just woken up. "Oh," she said, peering at me with drowsy, blinking eyes.

"Hi," I said.

"What are you doing here?"

The tone in her voice stung me. But I remained calm. "I was, uh . . . just walking around . . . ," I managed to say. "They let me off early . . . from the car wash."

"Oh," she said. I could see the house was dark inside, even though it was the afternoon.

"I wanted to see you," I said in a serious voice. "And I forgot to get your number. So I figured this was the best way."

She looked at me. She seemed unsure what to do. "Okay," she said.

"I can go," I said. "I just wanted . . . to say hi."

"No," she said. "It's all right. You can come in."

She opened the door more, and I stepped inside. She saw the scrape on my cheek. I had taken the Band-Aid off that morning.

"How's your face?" she asked.

"It's a lot better," I said, touching the scab. "Thanks for fixing me up."

She led me into her kitchen. She was wearing a man's shirt. No bra. Her thick black hair was sticking out on one side.

I looked around the kitchen. This was where we'd come the other night, after the fight. That had been the most thrilling night of my life. And here I was, back again.

"Uh . . . so . . . yeah," said Phoebe, scratching her head. She looked at me. "Do you want a beer? Or some coffee?"

"Coffee'd be good," I said.

As usual, my eyes followed her around the room. There was a slowness to her movements, but also a kind of composure, a controlled energy. I couldn't look away from her.

"So your mom's not home?" I asked.

She looked at me as if this was an odd question. "No," she said. She put two scoops of coffee in the machine and then poured water into it.

"What have you been up to?" I asked.

She shrugged. "Nothing much. Making T-shirts."

I didn't believe her, but I said nothing. I took a seat at the small table. Phoebe remained standing. As the coffee brewed, she cleaned up a little. She dumped out some ashtrays. Then cleared the counter of empty beer cans.

Eventually, she took a seat across from me at the table. She lit a cigarette. She hadn't really looked at me yet, but now she did. It was not an affectionate look. It was more like she was studying me. There was something going on with her. Did she want me there? Did she *not* want me there?

"This must be peak T-shirt-selling time," I said.

"Summer always is."

I nodded.

The coffee began to brew. She smoked. It still looked weird to me, someone that young smoking. Nobody at my high school smoked; that would be considered a sign that something was seriously wrong with you. In Seaside lots of people smoked. I didn't know what it meant.

"Do you ever worry," I said, "about cigarettes?"

"Like what? That they'll kill me?" she asked.

"Yeah. Or they say they make your skin bad."

"My skin . . . ?" she said, thinking about it. "No. I don't think about that."

The coffee maker began to gurgle. She stood and went to the cupboard and got two cups. She looked inside one of them. It must have been dirty, because she put it in the sink and then looked for another. She didn't seem to like any of the ones on the lower shelf, so she pushed up onto her tiptoes and reached for one on the next shelf up.

That was the moment. When she stretched upward. In her too-big man's shirt, and with her bare calves and bare feet and her arm stretched upward and her tangled mess of black hair.

I was up before I could stop myself, and then I had my arms around her, holding her from behind. She didn't react at first. She continued to hold the cups in her hands, while I buried my face in her neck and shoulder. I breathed in her hair. After I'd held and squeezed her for a moment, I released my grip. She put down the cups and turned to me and slid her hands up my chest and around my neck and kissed me deeply on the mouth. *So she does love me*, I thought. A tremendous surge of happiness poured through me. My soul felt like it was turning itself inside out. I wanted to give Phoebe all of myself, everything I had. I wanted to surrender to her completely.

"Come on," she said in a scratchy whisper. She took my hand and led me into her bedroom.

37

"There's so many things I want to tell you," I said. An hour had passed. I was lying on my stomach, in Phoebe's bed, half my head buried in a pillow. With my left eye, I watched the side of her face beside me.

Phoebe blinked several times, her thick black lashes fluttering like a tiny bird. "Oh God," she said. "You're not going to be like that, are you?"

"Like what?"

"Just . . . talking too much."

"No, I don't think so."

"Some people, they just talk talk talk," she said. "They can't shut up."

I stared at her with my one eye. What had gotten into her? "Yeah, but we just . . ."

"And then you'll want me to tell you things," she said. "Which I'm not going to do."

I continued to stare at her from my pillow. This was not the conversation I thought we were going to have. Maybe she got touchy after sex. She was like that the other time too. Maybe something traumatic had happened to her in her childhood. That seemed possible, with her mother never around, growing up in Seaside.

"No," I said as gently as I could. "I wasn't going to ask you anything."

She sighed. "It's nothing personal," she said. "But if you live in a tourist town, people come and go. You know? And you're going to leave soon, right? To go back to school or whatever?"

"Yeah."

"Are you in college?"

"High school. Senior year."

"I can never tell how old people are," she said. "I have a blind spot for that. Sometimes I can't tell anything about people."

"That's weird."

"Like Nicole? When she sees someone? She instantly knows all these things about them. It's like she's psychic."

"It's hard to know people sometimes," I said. "Even when you're around them a lot."

Phoebe looked down at her fingernails. "The thing about me is, there isn't anything to say." She looked at me with a sad expression.

I propped my head on my hand. "I bet there is," I said, running my fingers along her arm. "I'd want to know anything you felt like telling me."

"Like what?"

"Like . . . well . . . how you see things. And how you approach things. You're really funny sometimes. But other times more serious. And like your family. Where are they? What are they like?"

"My *family*?" she said, like that was the last thing she would ever talk about. She pushed the covers down and rolled off the bed. She walked naked to the bureau, where her phone was charging. She unplugged it and got back into the bed. "I have to check something," she said. "Do you mind?"

"No," I said.

She began scrolling on her phone, and I felt a sinking sensation in my chest. The presence of Phoebe's phone was never good. The attention she gave it, the way it lit up her face in the dark. I hated her phone. I was deeply jealous of it.

"I have to go soon," she said, turning it off and putting it beside her on the bedside table.

"Where are you going?" I asked.

She didn't answer. She pulled the covers up tight around her neck and closed her eyes.

"I'm sorry if I offended you," I said.

"You didn't offend me."

"I guess your family is your own business."

"I'm not offended," she repeated, without looking at me.

I couldn't think of what to say next. "Are you glad I came over?" I asked.

"Yes," she said. She turned and moved closer and began to snuggle with me. "Yes, I am."

She moved fully into my arms, which totally changed my thinking. The minute I felt her pressed against me, I was insanely happy again. I pulled her close and held her. I kissed her lips and caressed the sides of her face. The feeling of love was overwhelming. That was the thing about Phoebe: She seemed to *need* more love, and so somehow you *generated* more love. And all that extra love moving through you, it was like a drug, it was pure ecstasy, filling you up and then flowing into her, and then coming back to you again, creating this vortex of incredible bliss.

A half hour later we separated. She reached for her phone.

"Do you remember when I found you on the beach?" I said, after I'd caught my breath.

"No," she said, checking her messages.

"Really?" I said. I was on my back, staring at the ceiling. "After that first big party of the summer? At the Cove? Kyle was there. With Britney. You and Nicole were there."

She didn't answer.

"Anyway," I continued, mostly to myself. "I forgot my book on the beach and I went back early the next morning and I found you asleep on the sand. By yourself. Under an old sleeping bag."

"What?" she said, glancing at me once.

"I saw this old sleeping bag. And I thought it was just lying there. And I picked it up, and you were under it."

She frowned. "I don't think so."

"But it's true! You were asleep. Or passed out maybe. And I took you home."

She didn't respond.

"I'm totally serious," I said. "Do you not remember?"

"No," she said.

I looked at her then. "Wow," I said. "You really don't."

"You should probably go soon," she said to me.

"Okay," I said, but it was going to kill me to leave, to get out of that bed. I braced myself for the pain of it. I also wondered what she was doing later. And with whom. She hadn't told me. It was odd how sometimes she didn't answer when you asked her things.

I finally sat up, slid off the bed, and began to gather my clothes. "But just so you know," I said, pulling on my pants. "That really happened, finding you on the beach. Not that it matters. You were probably just really drunk."

"I don't know what you're talking about," she said.

"I'm sorry, but it's true. I found you. And I took you home."

She sighed. "I have to take a shower," she said. She got up and went into the bathroom.

I sat on the bed and put on my shoes.

It was dark when I went out the front door. I headed down the road toward the highway. It was the second time I'd

made that walk after being with Phoebe. It was as peaceful and profound as the first time: the quiet houses, the
single streetlamp, the dark sky above. And that deep sense
of completion and satisfaction in my body. Things had
definitely been more complicated tonight, but in the
larger picture that hardly made a difference. When you
really loved someone, and you connected with them, like
really connected with them, body and soul, something
happened. It was hard to describe exactly. But it was big.
It was life-changing.

But there was also the time problem. I was running out
of it. It was mid-August already. Maybe for this reason I
couldn't quite bring myself to continue toward the highway. After I'd gone a couple blocks, I stopped and turned
and went back. I guess that's how crazy for Phoebe I was. I
needed to stare at her house for a few more minutes.

The house across the street from hers had a big fir tree
in the front yard, and I sat under it, in the dark, leaning
my head back against the trunk. I could hear the ocean far
in the distance. A wet smoky haze drifted inland from the
beach.

Then a car came down the road. I quickly moved
around the tree so I wouldn't be seen. As it approached,
I saw it was Wyatt's Camaro. I stayed hidden, watching it
as it passed Phoebe's and parked on the corner. *So that's
who she's hanging out with tonight. Wyatt and Carson. Why
didn't she just say that?*

For a moment nothing happened. Then the driver's

door opened. Wyatt got out. He was wearing a Golden State Warriors jersey and a flat-brim hat. But where was Carson?

I watched Wyatt walk up the driveway of Phoebe's house. But instead of going to the front door, he ducked around the side of the house. There must have been a back entrance I didn't know about.

Once he was gone, the street went quiet again. Five minutes passed. Ten minutes. Twenty minutes. Slowly my brain began to comprehend what I was seeing. *So it wasn't Carson and Wyatt coming to take Phoebe out. It was just Wyatt . . . and he wasn't taking her out . . . they were staying in. . . .*

But what were they doing? My brain didn't want to think about that. A sinking feeling came into my chest. And not just a *sinking* feeling. A *sunk* feeling. A *game over* feeling. A *what the fuck* feeling.

I struggled to my feet. I needed to leave. I needed to get back to the Reillys' and the safety of my basement room. And then, as I stood, a new sensation came over me. A feeling of a strain I couldn't handle. A weight I couldn't hold. I was breaking inside. And then it happened. Something inside me actually broke. Some inner part of me seemed to collapse.

I staggered into the street as if I'd been shot.

I didn't sleep that night. At breakfast I sat at the table with Emily and Uncle Rob and Aunt Judy. Nobody talked. I pushed some eggs onto my fork and put them in my mouth. I forced myself to chew, and when I figured I'd chewed enough, I swallowed. I drank some orange juice and bit off a corner of my toast. There were pancakes but they looked dry, and I was afraid I wouldn't be able to swallow them.

At the Happy Bubble, I was slow and distracted. After lunch I began to come to my senses. I began to process what I'd seen outside Phoebe's house. By the end of my shift I'd straightened out certain facts in my head. The first was: *Phoebe had a boyfriend.* Okay. That made sense. She was super cute, and a million guys liked her. So no surprises there. The second was: *The boyfriend was Wyatt.*

This also made sense. He was a confident, good-looking (by Seaside standards) stoner guy who drove a Camaro, which, if I was honest with myself, was exactly the kind of guy you would expect Phoebe to be with. And then third: *But she also liked me.* That was correct too, I believed. I mean, I was a year younger than her, and not a badass like Wyatt. But I was okay-looking. And I was Kyle's cousin, which probably counted for something. Plus, we had slept together. Twice. And not only slept together, but talked and shared things and dozed in each other's arms. Something real had happened. Even if it was just a summer fling, Phoebe did care about me. Of course she did. And think how much I cared about her! I would have done anything for her. And I still would. Even after I'd seen Wyatt going into her house.

At home that night, after dinner, I ended up on the couch with Emily, watching *Dancing with the Stars*. She was texting a lot. Her life was starting to change now: Summer was winding down; Seaside High School would be starting soon.

I had my copy of *Letters to a Young Poet*. I still hadn't gotten past page twelve. I was trying to read it during the commercials. But I was too upset. I would occasionally get up and calmly go downstairs, where I would stomp around the basement and silently rage and fume. Then I'd come back up as if nothing had happened.

Then I remembered that Emily was friends with Wyatt.

Maybe she knew something about the situation. Maybe I could get some information out of her. And so, during the next commercial, I casually said: "Does that guy Wyatt have a girlfriend?"

Emily didn't answer right away. She was busy texting. "Wyatt?" she said. "I don't know. Probably."

"Justin was saying he saw him with Phoebe," I said, pretending to look at my book.

"Phoebe Garnet?"

"That's what he said. They seem like a good match."

Emily looked over at me. She was very perceptive. She could tell I was up to something.

"Do *you* know Phoebe?" she asked me.

"Me?" I said. "Sure. I mean, I've talked to her. She and Nicole come into the Happy Bubble sometimes."

"But you yourself? Have *you* talked to her?"

I shrugged. "Yeah. I ended up at her house once, with her and Nicole."

Emily lowered her phone and gave me her full attention. "You've been to Phoebe Garnet's *house*?"

"Yeah," I said casually. "What's so weird about that?"

Emily turned back to the TV. "Nothing."

I sat very still. I didn't say anything.

"What was her house like?" asked Emily.

"It was just a house. She and her mom make T-shirts and stuff. For tourists."

"What else do you know about Phoebe?" she said to the TV.

"Nothing," I said. "Just what everyone knows. She and Nicole. They're the life of the party."

"Yeah," said Emily. "That's true."

"I was just curious. Because Justin was saying—"

"*Are you in love with Phoebe Garnet?*" said Emily, turning toward me.

"Me?" I said. "No . . . I mean . . . I *like* her."

"Oh my God," said Emily, staring hard into my face. "You *are*."

"I wouldn't say that."

"Does Jace know about this?"

"There's nothing to know. I mean—"

"What exactly happened? Did you hook up with her?"

"Uh . . . well . . ."

"Oh my God," said Emily, turning back to the TV. "You hooked up with Phoebe!"

"It wasn't like that. I mean, we were drunk . . ."

"Of course you were drunk," said Emily. "She's always drunk." She stared at the TV without seeing it. "Do you think Phoebe loves you?"

This question seemed to stab into me. I looked at Emily. Why was she being so hostile about this? "I don't know . . . probably not . . . I mean, she *likes* me. She seems to enjoy my company."

Emily shook her head. She seemed physically pained by what I was telling her. She turned back to me. "Listen," she said. "Phoebe doesn't love you. You need to know that. Phoebe doesn't love anyone."

"What about Wyatt? She seems to love him."

"She doesn't. She doesn't love Wyatt. And she doesn't love you."

"But she must love somebody. . . ."

"No. She doesn't. She *can't*."

"Why can't she?"

"I don't know. And it doesn't matter!"

"Well, actually it does matter," I argued. "I mean, I know what you're saying. She's a tough girl. She's had a hard life—"

"Oh my God," said Emily, shaking her head.

"—but that doesn't mean she can't love somebody," I pleaded. "Everyone can love somebody. And if they don't have a person, they love their cat, or their dog. It's natural. People love. It's part of being human."

Emily stared at the TV. "Wow," she said. "She got you. She really got you. You're lucky you're leaving."

39

When I went to bed, I lay for a long time staring up at the wood beams and pipes.

Before tonight I'd assumed Phoebe and I would get together for some sort of final good-bye. Of course we would; you didn't have something as intense as we had, and then just vanish out of each other's lives. I'd imagined we would meet somewhere special. We'd talk, we'd feel sad together, but also we'd remember the fun we'd had and the feelings we'd shared.

Of course you did that. It would be heartless not to. And then you gave them one last hug and said good-bye and maybe shed a tear or whatever.

I'd been debating different locations for this final conversation. Phoebe and me on the Promenade, or sitting by a beach fire. I'd explain that I understood about Wyatt. He lived here. I did not. Obviously she and I could only be a temporary thing. I could accept that. But I would also tell her how much I loved her. I would do anything for her. I would help her in any way I could.

But now I wondered if I'd get a chance to say any of this. The whole situation had shifted so dramatically. I wasn't sure I understood Phoebe at all. It suddenly seemed possible I might never see her again.

For the next couple days I went to the Happy Bubble like always. I vacuumed. I cleaned. I ate stale donuts with Justin. I watched Mike smoke Marlboros in the back parking lot.

One day after my shift, I walked into town. I went to the coffee shop, where I stared at the pages of *Letters to a Young Poet* one more time. It was hopeless. I was never going to read this book. Maybe I didn't need the advice of some old German dude anyway.

I left the coffee shop and jammed the book in my back pocket. I walked down Main Street toward the Promenade. Summer was nearly over. There were still tourists around, but it was a different feeling. Main Street felt slower, less intense, a little melancholy. The beach had gotten colder, windier, blurrier. The sky didn't have that same midsummer brightness.

Of course the main thing in my brain was still Phoebe. I kept having this idea: *If you love her, fight for her.* But what did that mean, exactly? Get in a fight with Wyatt? Go bang on her door and demand something? What would I demand?

Fortunately, I had my real life to think about too. I was going back to Eugene soon. I needed to talk to my dad about scheduling. And I'd never called Dr. Snow back either. And what about my mom? What would happen with her when I got home? Would she want to see me on certain days? I was too old for that. I was done being "parented." At least by her. Plus, if Richard was around, what was I supposed to do with that? I mean, I barely knew the guy. And what I did know, I wanted to kill.

I continued to walk, lost in my thoughts. I found myself standing outside the Seaside Library.

I moved closer to the glass door and looked in. Jace was there, sitting behind the desk, scanning books. I swallowed once. I opened the door and went in.

When she saw me, a tight frown came onto her face. Emily had obviously told her about Phoebe and me.

"Hey," I said.

"Hey," she said, returning her eyes to her books.

I moved forward, toward her desk. "How's it going?" I said.

"Okay," said Jace. She kept scanning. When she was done, she stood and began putting the books in a cart and arranging them. "We're actually going to close in a few minutes," she said.

I nodded. I looked around the room. "Feel like going to the Sandpiper when you get off?"

She shook her head. "No, I have to help my mom."

"Help her do what?"

"Set up these cabinets she bought."

"Oh."

"Actually, they're more like bookshelves."

"Could I help?"

"No," she said quickly. "I mean, it's just moving some stuff around. We can handle it."

I nodded. She didn't want to hang out. That made sense. I thought I should go. But I couldn't seem to move. "Listen . . . Jace . . ."

She looked at me.

"I know things got sort of . . . ," I said. "I guess what I mean is, I'm sorry I didn't tell you how I felt . . . or what was happening. . . ."

She blushed slightly. She refocused on her books. "You don't have to say anything," she said. "I know about Phoebe. I understand. . . ."

I looked around the library some more. It was more of a children's library, I realized. A big poster on the wall showed a choo-choo train telling kids to read. There were stuffed animals in the storytelling corner and a miniature table and chairs.

"You've been through a lot," said Jace, still not looking at me. "Emily told me. I mean, not just about Phoebe. Before that. About your family and stuff. And your mom. She told me before you even got to Seaside."

"Yeah."

"Which was a mistake it turned out, because then I

liked you before I even met you. And then . . . well . . . you didn't like me back. Or not in the same way."

"But I did like you back," I said.

"Well, whatever. It doesn't matter now."

"I just got pulled off in a different direction."

Jace sighed. "Phoebe does that to people. I actually had a feeling that might happen. I was going to say something to you. I was going to warn you. But then I thought it wasn't any of my business. And you probably wouldn't have listened anyway. Nobody ever does."

I didn't know how to respond to that. I stood there, staring at the choo-choo train on the wall.

Jace began walking around, turning off the lights. She got out her keys. "I'm sorry, Nick. I have to lock up now."

I nodded and walked toward the door. I went outside but held the door open for a minute, waiting, thinking she might say something else, or say good-bye or something.

But she didn't. Instead she disappeared into the little office in back. So I let the door close and walked away.

I finally called my dad. I told him the bus schedule options for coming home—one bus left in the morning; the other left in the afternoon. We decided on the late one.

He didn't say anything about Mom. He seemed quiet in general and said he would update me when I got home. So I got off the phone and let him be.

On my last full day in Seaside, I went for a long walk on the beach and thought about Phoebe. I remembered all the way back to when she and Nicole first came into the Happy Bubble in the Jeep. How fun they seemed that day. Even grumpy Mike had left his post to join in. And then they'd come back a couple days later. That was the time Phoebe came into the office to use the restroom, and I'd moved aside to let her pass. In that moment, as our bodies nearly touched, I'd felt a part of me switch on. It was as if my soul had been searching for her soul, and had been for a long time. And here it was. Finally. Here *she* was.

And then the night of the party at the Cove, she and Nicole coming down the trail. Nicole yakking and screaming and waving to her admirers, while quieter, more mysterious Phoebe followed behind, picking her way down, not needing to call attention to herself. She appeared so delicate, so fragile, and yet she was actually not that way at all. Which was something I hadn't understood. And still didn't.

And then the fateful morning, which I'd replayed in my mind a hundred times. Finding her on the beach, lifting her up, holding her in my arms, already loving her, already protecting her, already wanting to be part of her crazy life. And the ride in the truck: that intoxicating mix of confusion and chaos and excitement and sympathy. *I can help you.* And then pulling into her driveway, and her still so out of it, and me so focused on her, so aware of her, so locked in on every detail of her being.

Why did I love her so much? This was the question. I barely knew her. You'd think sleeping with her would give me some idea who she really was, but that had only created an even more impenetrable wall between us. That was how she kept you away. By having sex with you. It was so backward from what you thought, from everything you'd ever been told about women and life and how love was supposed to work.

It was some trick she did. Some way of keeping herself hidden. By giving me the thing that guys always want, she slipped away, escaped into the ocean fog, vanished at the very moment I thought I'd possessed her. And oh my God, how I wanted to possess her. Still. Even now. Even when I knew better and had been warned and knew that nothing good could come of it. . . .

I walked for miles. Low clouds came in off the ocean, and a light rain began to fall. Still I continued, farther than I'd ever gone, beyond Gearhart, halfway to Tillicum.

When it really started to rain I turned around and went back. It was ten thirty by the time I got back to Gearhart and nearly midnight when I could see the soft lights of Seaside through the mist. I had vowed to not contact Phoebe before I left. I hadn't really embarrassed myself yet. I hadn't broken down or cried or acted pathetic in any way. If I kept to myself, I could leave with my dignity intact. If she'd wanted to see me, she could have found me easily enough. I was at the Happy Bubble every day. Unlike her, I was easy to locate.

But walking back along the northern section of the Promenade, I found myself drawn toward the narrow streets, which, if I followed them, would lead to Phoebe's house. I gradually veered in that direction and began taking the necessary lefts and rights. I passed the nicer houses closest to the ocean, and then the not-so-nice houses farther in. Junk in people's yards. Old tires. A metal bed frame. A rusting boat trailer. Sadness. Darkness. The whole of the world: It was all right there in Seaside.

My plan was to not stop. If I passed by Phoebe's but kept walking, nothing bad could happen. And technically this was a slightly faster route back to the Reillys'. And anyway, I was leaving the next day. Why not let Fate push me around as it would? What was I saving myself for?

I turned onto her street. My heart began to pound hard in my chest. My tired legs became springy with nervous energy. Her house appeared on my left, the roof drooping slightly, the screen on a front window ripped.

I slowed my pace to take in these details. I didn't want to linger or stare, but I also didn't want to rush by and not feel whatever emotions had driven me here.

As I slowed to a stop, I searched the front windows for signs of life. There didn't seem to be any. But that was the front of the house; the kitchen and Phoebe's bedroom were in the back.

Then I heard a banging sound. A screen door? It was from behind the house. I hurried across the street into the neighbor's yard, where I ducked behind that same tree. *Oh great*, I thought. *It's probably Wyatt again.*

But I didn't see the Camaro. I crouched behind the tree and watched the side of the house. I heard footsteps. It was so quiet I could hear the heavy breathing of whoever was coming out.

I kept still and waited. A large man appeared from the side of the house. He spit on the ground as he walked. It was not Wyatt. So who was it? As he turned down the street,

he reached into his overcoat and pulled out a pack of cigarettes. He put one in his mouth. I began to recognize these
movements. And then, when he stopped to light the cigarette, I knew exactly who it was.

It was Mike. From the Happy Bubble.

41

Aunt Judy took me to meet the Greyhound the next day.
The skies were gray and overcast. A few raindrops fell as we
drove along the highway. Aunt Judy switched on the wipers
for a moment, then switched them off.

It would have been nice if Emily had come, or Jace, but
apparently that wasn't happening. I thought about the other
people I might never see again: Justin. Kelsey. Even Kyle,
who might be whisked up into the fame and fortune of professional sports, never to be heard from again. And other stray
people: Tyler with his hippie dance. The bashful counter
girls at the Freezie Burger. Soft-hearted Billy Malone. And
then back to Justin, with his claw hand. Despite everything,
Justin had been a real friend to me. Even when I wasn't
much of a friend back.

But back to Emily and Jace. Had they totally dismissed

me now? For getting involved with Phoebe? That didn't seem right. How much can you help who you love and who you're attracted to? But in another way I understood. It was one of the lessons of Seaside. You had a choice: simple, solid relationships, where everyone understood each other and nothing much happened. Or something beyond that, something where you risked more and got more, and then eventually paid the price.

We waited in the car for the bus. I found myself staring at the FOR SALE sign in the abandoned gas station.

"So when does your school start?" Aunt Judy asked me.

"Next week. Tuesday, I think."

"Are you looking forward to your senior year?"

I didn't feel like talking. But I couldn't be rude. "Yeah, it should be fun."

"What electives will you be taking?"

"Spanish. And journalism."

"Journalism? That sounds interesting."

"Yeah, they have good journalism at my school."

Finally, the bus appeared, coming down the highway. The two of us stared at it. "I hope you had a good time with us this summer," said Aunt Judy.

"I did."

"And give your dad my best."

"I will," I said. "And thanks. Thanks for everything."

Aunt Judy stared forward. Her voice became serious. "You're always welcome here, Nick. I hope you know that.

No matter what happens. You always have a place to go. . . ."

I nodded that I understood. "Thanks, Aunt Judy."

The bus pulled in. I got out and lifted my rolling suit-case out of the back seat. I dragged it across the gravel. The bus driver came out and helped me slide it into the luggage compartment underneath.

Aunt Judy waited behind me and then gave me one last hug. She was starting to cry.

"Good-bye, Aunt Judy."

I got on the bus and found a seat by the window. The driver took his place at the wheel. There was a loud hiss as the brakes were released, and then the large bus lumbered back onto the road. I got out my book, *Letters to a Young Poet*, and opened it to the first section, the first page, the first sentence. But as usual, the print seemed to blur on the page. I couldn't absorb a word of it.

So I watched out the window instead. The outskirts of Seaside passed by. Within a minute or two the view changed to trees and mountains and the shallow river that followed along the highway.

I imagined myself then, driving a car on this same road, ten or twenty years in the future. I'd drive up from Eugene to visit my aunt and uncle. I'd be an adult, maybe a lawyer or a reporter, something like that. Naturally, it would be great fun to see everyone. Uncle Rob, Aunt Judy, whoever else was around. But after a few hours, I'd start thinking about Phoebe. Was she still here? What was she doing?

So then I'd drive into town and walk up Main Street,

asking at different places, "Is Phoebe Garnet still around?" Eventually someone would know her and direct me somewhere. Maybe she was a bartender at a local bar. So I'd go there, and walk in and there'd she be, older, a little worn down, but still attractive in an older person sort of way.

She'd be standing behind the bar, chewing on a straw, one of the regulars chattering on about some local gossip. There'd be no recognition, not at first. I'd order a beer and she would pour it, without noticing me. But then she'd glance up into my face, and see who I was. . . .

And then what would happen? Nothing, probably. She'd keep chewing on the straw. Maybe she'd say something. Maybe she wouldn't.

You wanted to think something lasted when you loved someone. Some part of that connection remained, that the person stayed inside you in a way. But maybe that wasn't always true. And maybe with someone like Phoebe, you didn't want them lingering on the outskirts of your heart, reminding you how unsafe the world was. Maybe it was better to forget some people completely. If you could. If that was even possible.

42

I got home at nine thirty that night. It felt good to get off the bus, to breathe the inland air, which was warmer, more earthy, more fragrant. Walking out of the bus station into downtown Eugene, I was struck by how clean and orderly the streets were. The expensive cars. The well-dressed people. Eugene was a college town. Everything was new and shiny.

My dad pulled up and popped the trunk, and I lifted my suitcase inside. I hadn't eaten, so we went to a new sandwich place that had opened down the block. It was very Eugene: The bread was organic; the produce locally grown. We sat by the window, while around us a scattering of college students talked or worked on their laptops. The academic life. It felt strange to be home.

*   *   *

I didn't know how long Phoebe would stay in my thoughts once I got settled. For the first day or two I continued to feel that same painful tightness in my chest. Not heartbreak exactly, more like a low-grade panic attack. I didn't sleep well. I forgot to eat. I couldn't seem to not think about her.

Part of the problem was I didn't have much to do, or anything else to focus on. I tried to keep busy running errands. I bought a new laptop from the Apple Store and some new Gap corduroys at the mall. I picked up my parking pass and locker combination from my high school.

At least I wasn't in Seaside anymore. And Eugene was so different. Even buying things seemed different. Here, you just whipped out your parents' credit card. It didn't matter what something cost. And the other young people around me, they seemed so confident and pleased with themselves, as if they'd done something spectacular just by being alive.

Then Kate called. "You've been home for three days?" she said. "Why didn't you call me?"

I could hear the concern in her voice. She had been worried about me, I realized.

She invited me over to Edith's, who was having a pool party since her mom was out of town. So I drove over there. Edith was making piña coladas and gave me one, and I took my place beside the pool. Other friends of ours were there, and I got to hear about everyone's trips and the people they met and the other news of the summer.

"Nick was in Seaside," said Kate at one point. "Working at his uncle's car wash."

Everyone looked at me with amazement.

"A car wash?" asked Edith. "What was that like?"

"It was okay," I said.

"Did you at least meet some girls?" asked Josh.

"A few. Here and there," I said.

"Oh my God. But Seaside is so *skanky!*" said Libby Baldwin.

"I know," said Edith. "All those arcades. And the creepy locals."

"And everyone is so fat," added Libby, as she sucked on her straw.

"Libby!"

"What?" she said. "It's true. They eat too much fried foods!"

"We went there once," said Chloe Edelman. "And the hotel was so awful my parents refused to stay in it."

"I didn't mind it," I said, taking a sip of my piña colada. "It was different. It was a learning experience."

"Yeah, learning to be poor!" said Edith.

"Oh my God!" said Libby. "Did you hear about Gigi? And her counselor at tennis camp?"

The conversation quickly turned to Gigi and her tennis-camp romance. Which got me off the hook. Which was good.

* * *

Once school got going, that's when I felt the first change in my feelings about Phoebe. My thoughts and memories of her seemed to shift into a slightly more remote place in my mind. She wasn't the first thing I thought about when I woke up. Or the first image that came to mind when I was alone somewhere. I still had days when I couldn't shake the hurt she had left in me. I felt "gutted" was what I told Dr. Snow. On those days I found myself going back to the questions that were never answered: What caused her to be like she was? What would happen to her? Had she cared about me at all?

But on most days, being a senior, I had more urgent things to worry about: Class assignments. College applications. Prepping for my SATs. But even then, after a long night studying in the library, I would be packing up my stuff and realize that the memory of Phoebe had been hovering around me like a ghost. The walk home would turn into one more imaginary conversation with her, one last attempt to clarify what exactly had happened between us. Other times I would find myself trying to explain it to some future girl-friend or wife: *The summer I was seventeen, I met this girl . . .*

And then there were the times when I *wanted* to remember her. When I actually *craved* that gnawing pain in my chest. Sometimes I would ride my bike for miles and let Phoebe come to me, and be inside me, and hurt me again. Which felt strangely satisfying and seemed to cleanse me in some way.

*   *   *

In general, though, the more time passed the better things got. Having my mom living in her own apartment turned out to be a huge relief. And my dad was actually in better shape mentally than when I left. He seemed genuinely happy for a change. Maybe he'd given up and was finally moving on.

And my mom. Oh my God. I don't even want to tell this part, but I guess I have to. It turned out my mom had kept a journal throughout her troubles, starting with her first DUI arrest six years before. Without telling anyone, she'd carefully recorded everything: the rehabs, the relapses, the affairs. She'd turned this journal into a memoir and sold it to her book publisher for a shitload of money. They were already planning the book tour. This was a hard thing for me to digest. MOM WINS AGAIN! But as Kate pointed out, it was probably for the best. The thing with my mother was, if all the attention was on her, she was happy. And when she was happy, she left the rest of us alone.

And then one cold morning in November I was sitting in senior history class when I got an unexpected text.

Hey Nick, I wanted to let you know that I'm coming to Eugene tomorrow to take a tour of University of Oregon. It is currently my number one school, because it's not too far away and my counselor says I can get good financial aid. Are you there? Would you want to hang out? I also wanted to thank you for telling me about colleges that time on the beach. That really helped me. Jace

I waited for Jace inside the university student center. I was pretty nervous to see her again. It had been three months. And now she would see me how I really was, not like how I'd been over the summer, trying to fit in at the Happy Bubble.

But the moment I saw her, I knew everything was okay. She seemed thrilled to be there, in Eugene, at a big university, and to have a real friend to talk about it with.

She was with her mother, who I hadn't met. I was surprised by her mom. She was neatly dressed and totally smart and nice, not like Jace described her, as this uneducated person who couldn't go to the Pacific Grill.

They had already been on the official campus tour, so the three of us got smoothies and talked. I told them a little bit about my mother's life as a professor, and about her new book.

"Nick wants to be a writer too," Jace told her mom.

I shrugged and said, "I'm thinking about it."

After a while Jace's mom went back to their hotel, and Jace and I walked around to some of the places they hadn't shown her on the tour.

I took her to the Collective, which was this art gallery/ coffee shop place off campus where they had poetry readings and music. Then we checked out the basement of the student center where they had cheap snacks at all hours, and you could play pool or do karaoke. Then we went to the student lounge in the big library, which was one of my favorite places to hang out. It was open late, and you could study or read or just sit around with the college kids and feel like you were in college yourself. Jace really liked that. She liked everything about the university. In that way she and I were the same. We both loved the student life.

Jace and her mom were leaving early the next day, so we hung out in the library lounge as long as we could. We got hot chocolates out of the coffee machine and lay back on the couches and talked. There was no mention of Phoebe or Seaside or Emily. Now it was all about the future, our future, where we hoped to go, and what we hoped to do.

After that I walked Jace back to her hotel. It got a little awkward, saying good-bye in the lobby. I finally gave her a hug. This started as a "friends" hug, as a "let's stay in touch" hug. But once I had my arms around her, I couldn't seem to let go. All these feelings came flooding over me.

Tears filled my eyes. Jace was such a hopeful person. And I needed that hope. I needed it bad.

She didn't seem to mind. She seemed willing to stand there for as long as it took. So I settled my head on her shoulder. And I held her. And I held her. And I held her.

Acknowledgments

Many thanks to Liesa Abrams, Jessica Smith, and everyone at Simon Pulse. And to Jodi Reamer and Alec Shane at Writers House. Special thanks to invaluable readers: Jenny Altshuler, Laural Winter, Kevin Samuels, Celina Amaya, Paula Nelson, Penny Nelson. (Teenage) relatives whom I pester for information: Noah Nelson, Orion Wiebe, Cassandra and Vivian Wiebe, Misha Hindery, James Hindery. Other friends and advisors: David Colton, Steve Arndt, Sarah Pearlman, Lidia Yuknavitch, Liz Mehl, Gabe Cohen, Kari Luna, April Henry, Claire Dederer, Rachel Rifkin, Christa Desir, Renee Steinke, Natalie Standiford, Melissa Walker, Gayle Foreman, Nick Tucker, Peter Drake, Adam Weiss, Martha Grover, Jen Ziegler, Jason Etemad-Lehmer, Mary Suzanne Garvey, Laura Locker, Melissa Locker, Vanessa Gallagher, Kari Luna, Jesse Sposato, Alex Simpson, Chelsea Hogan, Nancy Petriello Barile, David Gutowski, Kevin Sampsell, Michelle and family (and everyone) at Seaside Coffee House.

BLAKE NELSON

is the author of many young adult novels, including *Recovery Road* (now a TV series), the coming-of-age classic *Girl*, *Boy*, and *Paranoid Park*, which was made into a film by Gus Van Sant. He lives in Portland, Oregon.